OLD FARMHOUSES OF THE NORTH

MICHELLE VON ESCHEN

978-1-7376875-8-0

PRAISE FOR MICHELLE VON ESCHEN'S WORKS

"HEARTFELT, INTELLIGENT, DARKLY POETIC, AND BEAUTIFULLY
FIGURATIVE WHILE ALSO BEING ECONOMICAL."
-TYLOR JAMES, AUTHOR OF MATTERS MOST MACABRE

"VON ESCHEN CRAFTS HAUNTING SHORT STORIES OF QUIET
HORROR THROUGH THE LENS OF LOSS AND GRIEF . . . [SHE] HAS
A FANTASTIC SENSE OF PACING."
-BOB FOSTER, CITY OF GEEK

"AS A FELLOW WRITER AND PUBLISHER, GENERALLY FULL OF
CONFIDENCE, MICHELLE IS ONE OF THOSE AUTHORS WHOSE
STELLAR WRITING TEMPORARILY SHAKES MY FAITH IN MY OWN.
SHE'S THAT GOOD."
-JONATHAN LAMBERT, AUTHOR OF GUGGA AND BETWIXT THE DARK
& LIGHT: A COLLECTION OF ODDITIES

"[MICHELLE'S] WRITING WILL EMOTIONALLY CRUSH YOU AND
PHYSICALLY DESTROY YOU. AND YOU COME BACK, ASKING FOR
MORE."
-T.J. TRANCHELL, AUTHOR OF CRY DOWN DARK AND TELL NO MAN

"SLICK AND CLEVER..."
-PETER CLINES, AUTHOR OF THE FOLD, THE EX-HEROES SERIES,
AND PARADOX BOUND

Dedicated to those after something more.

And to Jonathan who, for me, is just that.

OLD FARMHOUSES OF THE NORTH

MICHELLE VON ESCHEN

CONTENTS

> "IN ORDER TO INDUCE THE PROCESS OF DECAY, WATER
> IS NECESSARY. I THINK THAT, IN THE CASE OF
> WOMEN, MEN ARE THE WATER."
> -NATSUO KIRINO, GROTESQUE

OLD FARMHOUSES OF THE NORTH

She rests her head against the rain-covered window of the pickup truck. Her face is mostly turned away from him. He sneaks glances at what he can see of her–her flickering left eyelid, one of her knees, the pale and perfect skin of her collarbone.

When the road isn't too rough, he takes a hand from the wheel to touch her black hair. She's quiet for most of the drive, save for the thump of her head as it bounces off and returns to the glass with every bump in the road, save for the occasional chatter of her teeth. The thin blanket on her lap is no match for the cold so the man turns on the heat–a pitiful hint of warm air leaking out of the vents on the cracked dashboard–that cools before reaching her skin.

When a woman is yours, you keep her warm, he thinks. But the moving air makes things worse for her, causes shivers so hard she's bitten her tongue. Out of the corner of his eye, he sees the red of a small trickle of blood leaking from between her blueing lips. He leans for the handle of the glove compartment.

When a woman is yours, you help her, he thinks as he gropes into the void for a napkin. He wipes her chin, careful not to rouse her or disrupt the pink shade smeared on her lips.

The truck crosses the southern border of the north. When the winters became so harsh and long that the crops couldn't recover, the families abandoned everything. Their land and their homes, their livelihoods. The first of those empty farmhouses appears. There, at the corner of its yard, something foreign protrudes from the ground, ground nothing much has grown from in a decade. The *For Sale* sign invites in him a gripping, momentary fear that dissipates when he reminds himself that no one wants to live this far away from anything living. The farmhouse will sit on the market until, like the house, the sign falls apart, until the real estate agent comes to slap a *Price Now Reduced!* decal to its front, testing the strength of the rusted chains and its post, split from top to the ground like a lightning-struck tree, sternum to pubic bone like a cadaver. The cost drop was little more than an industry-accepted form of life support, an intubation for an oxygen-deprived market, a physical proof that everything had been done to make the house a home once more.

He looks over at her again. "You can tell just by looking at it, it's not the one. No. It's still a drive from here."

Even if a prospective buyer came and found value in the low price, the man knows the house belongs to someone else, someone his passenger can never know about. Someone who sat in her seat before her.

When a woman is yours, you make her feel like she's the only woman in the world, he thinks. *Erika*, he reminisces privately.

He recalls the brown of the dead wheat in the field behind the first farmhouse, the chestnut fur of the mice living in the walls, the elm hardwood throughout the first floor, life-worn and faded. Erika's hair was watered down whiskey and her skin, a lightened terracotta. She fit the muted brown tones of the house and its surrounds so well; it made sense she'd end up there with him. It felt like the house had been built for her before her birth, expecting her eventual arrival. Erika is encased in the wall of the mudroom, her arms crossed over her chest like an Egyptian queen, still smelling of his emissions were it not for the overpowering stink of her decay.

The house passes and shrinks in the rear view mirror. Still his passenger shivers. He hopes she's fallen asleep, but more likely she's awake and it's the anger keeping her silent. She protested at first, hours ago, at the beginning of the drive, not wanting to head North where nothing existed anymore. "There's nothing up there," she said, like so many of the others said before her. As though it would change his mind. As though it might save their lives.

They pass another farmhouse. One with a giant, red barn the exact shade of Tara's hair. Strawberries once grew in its fields, according to the weathered sign, and were free to anyone willing to pick them. When he was done with her, he folded Tara in half and buried her in the oversized cherry-colored planter beneath the kitchen window. He thinks of stopping to see if life has sprung from the microbial wealth of her dead body. Maybe on the way back, once he delivers his new passenger home.

When a woman is quiet, you make small talk, he thinks, because her silence is wearing on him. His hands grip the wheel. He wants to say something to break through the desolate cavern of unsaid things between them, even just a word or two to cut through the sound of the tires negotiating with the gravel of the road. Her bare legs distract him and the unblemished blanket of her pale skin steals any words he might have found. Her perfection almost drives the truck into the ditch.

He doesn't like to think of Christal, the one who almost got away, the one who tore him to shreds before succumbing to her wounds, but there's only one road through the farmland and her house looms next on the drive. It's a modern build of an imposing three stories with thick columns lining the wraparound deck and horse stables backing the property. He'd picked it for her for its durability, its sturdiness, and for the strength of the horses that used to roam the land. The siding was unscathed by the harsh weather, just as Christal appeared untouched by the streets she let touch her. He'd had to beat her in a fight for his own life when taking hers and that left her corpse bruised and swollen. Finally conquered, she lays in a stall of the stable, mixing with the hay.

The weather is terrible. Sheets of rain, with the help of the wind, efficiently soak the landscape. A recognizable landmark pops up on the distant horizon and he knows they've nearly arrived. He wants her to see the large grain silo so he reaches over and pries open her eyelids. Still she's unresponsive or perhaps unimpressed by the grandeur of the structure.

When a woman is yours, you call her by her name, he thinks.

He thought he knew it, but digging through his mind doesn't turn it up so he digs in her purse sitting between them on the tattered pleather of the bench seat. He drives with one hand, fighting the drag and pull of the deep roadside puddles. The uneven ride does not concern her. Amid receipts, tampons, and lipstick, his hand finds the hard plastic of her license.

He brings the card to the top of the wheel and places its edge in the ditch of the stitching to make out her moniker.

"Wynter. That's right."

When she told it to him, he figured it was spelled like the season, not knowing there was any other way to arrange letters into the same sound. She looks old in her picture, like she put on too much makeup for the DMV photo, like she stole her mother's ID to get into the bar where he found her. Maybe the girl sitting next to him isn't even legal. It doesn't matter either way. She's perfect. She's exactly what he was looking for.

More farmhouses pass and he recalls the names of the women he's brought to them. Miranda and Lilliana, April and Linda. Others too, whose faces he can see, but whose names he has forgotten over time.

Wynter whimpers and it pains him.

When a woman is yours, you take away all her worries, he thinks.

"It's just up the road. Hold on. We're almost there."

He followed everything his father taught him, all the rules to treat a woman right, but he kept getting it wrong. It was his dream to carry a dying woman over the threshold of her home and to watch her take her final breath inside where they could share the perfectness of the place. But the timing has always been off. Blood no longer seeps from Wynter's head wound. Her left eyelid flickers less often now. He can't be certain she's seeing much of the not much that's out there, the wheat whipping by, the farmland stretching in all directions, unwatched and purposeless, feeding only his quest for solitude and uninterrupted contentment.

"Don't go yet! Don't go," he yells. That was the trouble with these drives up North. The women often didn't survive the trip, forcing him to rush his plans, eat his dinner cold and hard, or leave the table altogether before the feasting was finished. He depresses the accelerator and listens to the roar of the engine as it drowns out her final rattles.

They arrive at the farmhouse and he remembers why he selected Wynter to rot inside its walls. Her hair is as black as the steel, cobweb-filled mailbox half-buried in thriving weeds at the start of the driveway and as dark as the stagnant, bacteria-laden water at the bottom of the stone well in the side yard. Her lips were the same pale pink of the fabric banner hanging from the porch that reads 'Home Sweet Home'.

He pulls the truck to the side of the road and walks around to the passenger door to tap on the glass where her nose smooshes against it. Wynter stares through the glass and through him, her eyes a cool blue, not unlike the sky above the grey clouds. Her breath no longer fogs up the window, but the rain runs droplets of water down the surface, suggesting she might be crying about the circumstances. Ice crusts the handle and sears his palm as he opens the door.

"We're here." His deep voice batters her still form, like crashing waves on an otherwise quiet coastline. He scoops her up like a sleeping child. There's wetness underneath her and he grimaces when he realizes he forgot to put any plastic down. It's sloppy and sloppy will get him caught sooner than his work will be done. Her feet catch on the edge of the doorframe and he raises her higher to beat the barrier there. An empty chip bag clings to one of her shoes and releases to find a spot on the ground outside. He doesn't think to pick it up. It'll blow away on the wind, a plastic tumbleweed lost to the distance.

The tailgate squeaks as the rusty hinges are asked to move. He lays her down on the metal bed. Her open eyes and the slack edges of her mouth give an impression of happiness. For a moment, she is not a new corpse, but a carefree girl watching the clouds pass. She stares at the sky as he undresses her. Her clothes pull off easily enough, now that any resistance has ended.

Her skin is as pale an eggshell as the chipped paint of the truck. From above, she blends in with her surroundings as though she was born to lie there, nude and dead. Her ring of black hair could be a spare tire or a garbage bag and the hair on her pubic bone, a clump of dark moss or dirt. Her nipples, two washers from a repair job. Only the blue of her eyes and the pink still lingering on her lips betray her location.

He feels for the bump on her head where the baseball bat made his most recent dream come true. The only imperfection on her body is luckily hidden by her thick hair. His shoulder burns from the home run swing, a muscle tear his activity has not allowed to heal.

In the beginning, when he'd killed his first and the crops had only recently started to die, other men would visit the north on occasion. They'd pray at the edges of the fields for a new yield to save their farm and families, and they'd gather their belongings in defeat when nothing came out of the ground. The visits slowed and eventually stopped altogether until the desperate real estate agents flew in to circle the corpses of the countryside, looking for salvageable meat in the market.

He stands to survey their surroundings for any movement. Save for the rustling trees, a few crows picking at something in the road a ways ahead, and a swinging shutter on the house beside them, the world is still.

Satisfied they are alone, he grabs her feet and pulls her from the truck bed. He throws her body over his good shoulder like a sack of wheat, a bounty he has harvested. The frozen grass crunches under his boots as they carve a crooked path toward the house.

Her now ashen skin nearly matches the weathered wood siding. He could sit her up against it and her encroaching greys would mix and meld with the dusty silvers until she'd be indistinguishable from the structure. His true work is inside, however, so he opens the front door, its lock as useless as the soil, and carries Wynter over the threshold as a husband might his new bride.

If you give a woman a house, she'll make it a home, he thinks.

Rot eats through the floorboards, a reminder that his time with Wynter is temporary. Lace curtains cling desperately to rusting poles in the living room and kitchen. He pictures her in the rooms, when sunlight still barreled through the windows and before the furnishings were packed up and taken away. She's so young his daydream will be her only taste of such domesticity. She will never be a day older than this.

He carries her through the first floor rooms the rats have claimed, careful to avoid the piles of droppings scattered about the decaying hardwood. There's a rhythm to his movements, a petite waltz of perfectly selected steps as he dances lead to the stairwell. Without intending to, she gives weight as he spins. Her dead heaviness propels them up the first step. The momentum doesn't last as his knees begin to moan under the realization of her true weight in death. He steps gingerly, having fallen through steps in other houses, houses not faring as well as this one. Sometimes the weather gets in the windows. Sometimes it eats everything up just enough for it to start falling apart on its own.

He picks the largest of the rooms, empty but for a full-length mirror propped in a corner. Tributaries of cracking etch the glass and flakes of silver backing peel and shed, making tiny windows through the reflection, losing its potential by the day. He places Wynter's corpse in the middle of the room where it's losing its potential by the minute.

He undresses himself and folds his clothes neatly beside the girl. Wynter waits with the unending patience only a corpse can offer as he examines his own body. Sun and age have spotted his skin and left it dry and wrinkled. A few bruises form colorful nebula on his arms and sides, testament to the struggle she put up. He feels unstoppable, only slightly marred while the woman lies dead behind him.

He crouches, bent in silent worship at the slowly crumbling church of her. The cold of the floor eats at the thin skin of his knees. Undecided about where to begin adoring her body, he leans forward and his lips drop to her belly.

When a woman is yours, you can do as you please with her, he thinks.

The man contorts her to his liking, pulls strings and rigging in his mind to move his marionette. She follows his commands without protest. He moves her closer to the mirror and yanks on her dark hair to lift her head. Her eyes no longer focus on anything. Her mouth hangs agape.

Hours pass as he uses her body to pleasure himself. Over and over he falls in love with her as her slack mouth takes in his full length, as her jaw never locks, as she never gags, as he moves from hole to hole and she never complains. His tiring hips push harder into her crotch as rigor mortis reaches the nearby tissue, causing a lifelike sensation of her clenching his circumference. The tightening sends him over the edge one final time and he releases his seed into her pointless womb. The house feels alive.

His imagination can't compete with the rigor as it steals her remaining lifelike-flexibility. He could wait it out, but the frost is finding him all the same. She looks beautiful in the center of the room so he dresses and leaves her there. The day is already taking a turn toward evening as he walks to his truck.

He stuffs her belongings into a garbage bag and places it onto the seat beside him for the drive back to the silo. It feels less lonely that way, with the black mound of plastic in his peripheral vision, riding shotgun as she had on the way in.

His shoulder aches as he climbs the small ladder up the silo's side and his legs feel weak from all the crawling around he did on the hardwood. The plastic bundle she's been reduced to is tied across his body with a rope. It bounces and twists as it dangles.

At the top, he opens the hatch and drops the sack into the darkness. Out of sight, it lands with a *clomph* on a small mountain of identical packages. One day maybe he'll dump gasoline inside and make the thing an oven, erase what the animals and insects won't take away, but he isn't yet ready to say goodbye so completely by drawing attention to his acts.

He closes the hatch and looks out into the rolling fog at the farmhouses in the distance as they fade in and out of visibility, knowing who lies in each one, knowing the ones still in need of an occupant and the urge once more rises inside him to find a pairing, a match, a forever home for a forever lover. Tears gather in his eyes, but only from the sharpness of the biting wind.

"Hello!" he calls out to his wasting harem. Only the wolves and the worms answer back.

WHAT TO EXPECT WHEN YOU'RE EXPECTING

I didn't want to be a mother. I'd decided that when I was a kid, as my own mother couldn't keep her eyes open to enjoy the dinners she'd slaved over. It was hard work, parenting, or maybe I was a difficult child. Either way, I wasn't interested in a life of exhaustion and definitely not missed meals, but then I met Mark and my mind changed almost overnight. A child would be a further expression of our love, another outlet to demonstrate the bond between us. Two wasn't enough anymore. It was time to expand, decorate a nursery, nest, devote every waking moment to new life. It was time to invite the weariness home to stay.

We tried for a year and a half, an effort exhausting in its own right, and where a baby didn't grow, there implanted frustration and a need to prove my aging body wrong. *We can do this!* I'd whisper to it. A whisper barely audible over the cacophonous ticking of my biological clock.

First Trimester - When it finally did happen, Mark kept

the pregnancy test until we saw the baby on an ultrasound, as though tossing the stick in the trash might somehow negate the biological efforts of our bodies and render me childless once more. I didn't blame him. I wanted to spend nine months at the clinic, lubed up, watching the child grow on the monitor like some slow burn human equivalent of waiting for water to boil.

Isn't it true how everything happens at once? We'd been looking to move from our apartment into a house, one with enough room for the three of us, but few options existed within the growing city and our shrinking budget. Turns out babies were expensive, even before they came out of you.

"What about a farmhouse?" Mark asks over coffee one morning. "One far from all the chaos and crime?"

"We can't afford a farm."

"We can. One without animals. Without anything." He tosses the newspaper onto the table in front of me, on a page with dozens of completely affordable farmhouses in varying states of disrepair.

"Why are they so cheap? These lots are huge."

"Nothing grows there anymore. The dirt's infertile."

The word still stings, even though we're beyond it. Mark catches my discomfort and keeps talking.

"It's not far from here either. We just need to pick one that doesn't need as much work. Cautious optimism, babe."

We make the drive up to meet the agent at a listing, getting lost several times because the navigation can't be convinced that anyone would choose to go where we're going. The robotic voice demands we make a U-turn at our next convenience, as soon as possible, before it's too late. Mark yells back there's only one way North. I silently scream that this is a place to dump bodies not start a family, but forward is forward and whether there's a forever home or a grave at the end, at least I'll be able to lie down.

Hulking farm machinery rusts at the far corners of the landscape, holding down the otherwise empty fields as though they might completely blow away in the wind. Just as much a part of the ruins, the barns and stables scream for purpose as the gales smack against the weakening wood. Eventually, the house looms on the gray horizon just behind a battered windbreak of Blue Spruce. I commiserate with the trees, pushed so far in one direction, under pressure to hold everything together.

The agent beams as she steps onto the gravel drive, taking in the vast amounts of absolutely nothing. I'm not smiling. I can barely breathe. Country life, in relentless gusts, is being crammed down my throat.

"There's hardly any traffic!"

"It's abandoned!" I yell into the wind.

Mark smacks my shoulder. I suppose it's inappropriate to undermine the agent's clever spins on the property's inadequacies. She's trying. We've only just arrived.

"This is the southernmost border of the Northern Zone. You'd own a piece of history. The last pioneers of a now untrodden land."

I'll give her that. It *looks* like history, every dusty, rotting, falling off piece. The shutters cling for dear life to the weather-beaten siding, the porch sinks on one side, threatening to rejoin the landscape. It's a far cry from the house with all the right angles pictured in the real estate listing. A skinny cat emerges from behind the house and runs to my side, mewing for the food it expects I might have. Mark runs deeper into the yard.

"This place is amazing, babe. Look at all this open space. It's perfect for a dog!"

"Don't push it. I'll never be a dog person."

The cat follows me to the front door.

"Well I hope you like cats. This one seems to come with the house!"

"I haven't even said I like the house."

Inside, our breath hangs in clouds, vaporous specters haunting rooms long after we tour them. Mark catches me observing the phenomenon.

"We'll double the insulation, get those extra thick windows, and wear socks to bed."

"What about the baby?"

I imagine her in a pink snowsuit. One so puffy she can't move her limbs. She'll lie in her crib like a starfish clinging to a rock, a tiny, spread-eagled god sacrificed on an invisible cross for the sake of cheap rent.

"Kids are resilient," the agent says with a knowing laugh. I look closer at her and recognize something. It's weariness chic. The bags under her eyes hang lower than the shutters, her breasts are as used up as the soil, dust from dry shampoo smatters her thinning hairline. She's a mother and a glimpse of my future.

"They survive a lot," Mark agrees.

"Not hypothermia! Come on, are we really considering this?"

I know his answer by the look on his face. He's impressed by the agent's conviction in defending the frozen circles of hell she's leading us through. The kitchen, living room, the bonus room, each one colder than the next, and each one presented in order as spacious, open and airy, and great in the summertime. The master bedroom, with its drafty walls, is positively titillating, meaning my nipples are hard as rocks from the bite.

"Should we show her the nursery?"

Mark and the agent make eye contact, betraying their plans. I knew it. They're conspiring against me, saving the best for last, fixing a failed dinner with a perfected dessert.

I'm given the uneasy pleasure of opening the last door at the end of the second floor hall. I turn the handle with a trepidation reserved for a jack-in-the-box. My teeth chatter. I expect to see raccoons or the bodies of pigeons. I expect to see Satan himself protruding from the frozen puddle in the center of the floor, evidence of our arrival to the very pit of hell and a leak in the roof we'll need to address. Instead I see the view and it's one for which I'll risk frostbite.

"Wow."

A picture window makes up the entire far wall, framing the farmland into a timeless agricultural painting of muted hues and breathtaking peacefulness. Mark skirts the mini ice rink and stands beside me.

"I knew you'd love it. Couldn't you just stand here forever?"

"Until the cows come home."

"Someday perhaps the cows migh-"

Mark stops the agent with a visible gesture of a hand slicing his neck. My hesitancy drops with the cut and the room with a view sells me on the place.

"We'll take it. We'll make it work."

My husband can't ever claim I'm not convincible.

There are things such as space heaters and changes of heart.

A month later, after the difficult intricacies of escrow and estrogen, we sit on the bare floor of the future nursery and prepare to name our child. Mark looks overwhelmed by the task.

"Do we really need three books?"

"The baby needs a name."

"Yes. One. Only one name," Mark reminds me as he holds the thickest of the books. "This one has three thousand names, it's probably in here somewhere."

"Well, our baby needs two names, technically. A first and a middle and children grow into their names so it's a huge choice. We're determining a future here."

"Or naming a serial killer."

"Are you going to help or what?"

My head's down. He doesn't answer. He's already in another room doing something easier, like watching paint dry. I start at the beginning, with the A's, and I don't get very far. Ava, 'a wished for child'. She doesn't even need a middle name. The first one is perfect.

At some point Mark allows the cat inside and it never leaves. He's the color of dirt and even though I have books full of names, Dirt sounds fine to me. Mark vows to call him Mud when he's wet. Not yet a dad and already making dad jokes.

My anxiety runs high during the first trimester. The stink of old memories at the apartment, the fumes of the repair work and the heavy scent of brewed coffee at the farmhouse all snake into my nostrils and threaten to cause a miscarriage. Fever dreams of an asbestos-ridden birthing suite wake me to my own ferocious scratching of my skin. I want out of the apartment, out of my pregnant body. I pack and empty boxes as often as my stomach, as the morning and moving sickness take hold.

Second Trimester - Things begin to resemble normal during the second trimester. My morning sickness leaves about the same time as we turn in the keys to our old place. Everything is unpacked and tucked away in its new home, including my fears, which have been pushed into a hall closet with the vacuum cleaner. Everything is fine until Dirt cries in the middle of the night, so loud I wake and search the farmhouse for the logic and location of his sorrow. He's in the nursery, staring out the big picture window, howling at something hovering above the fields, brighter and bigger than the moon. It's definitely not the cows returning and through the frame, I feel like I'm watching a movie.

"I don't like the look of it either." I talk to him, but he doesn't respond to my voice, instead he weaves a nervous path between my legs, carrying on with his petite air raid siren all the while.

The light brightens until the shapes of the house around me disappear. A beam emanates from the center of the shape, a laser pointer so large, the cat dares not seek its capture. In the dark safety of my womb, Ava moves as the ray penetrates, as though she's trying to hide from whatever intrusion we're experiencing. I feel a growing heat at my center. The bun in my oven is on fire.

"Mark!" His name departs with the strength in my legs and my consciousness.

I wake on the floor of the nursery to Dirt shrieking at me from the doorway, to something silkier than my nightgown gliding between my legs. Blood. Not enough to rush to the hospital, but certainly enough to send me into a fit of panic-calling my gynecologist until the incessant ringing of her phone rouses her. The thing in the field is gone. The room is dark again. My oven is cool. Mark is trying to get by Dirt, who refuses to let him close to me. I don't know how I got my cellphone. Maybe the pregnancy is making me insane. Maybe the paint is taking brain cells for strength as it dries.

"Hello?"

I barely hear the greeting over the hissing of the cat. I tell her what I remember, but it sounds a bit too *Close Encounters of the Third Kind* as it comes out of my mouth. Mark is hearing it for the first time too.

"Put her on speaker."

I do.

"The changing hormone and stress levels can create a breeding ground for nightmarish thoughts. It's common during pregnancy. I'm sure nothing is wrong."

"Nothing *can* go wrong! The walls are painted! We just built the crib!"

"She has a name!" Mark adds in the background where he now struggles to hold the still hissing Dirt.

"How do you feel now? How much blood would you say it was if you could scoop it all up into a measuring spoon? A tablespoon? More?"

"I hadn't thought of collecting it."

"Right, but if you had, how much would it be?"

I look at the stain on the carpet, lift my nightgown and examine my inner legs.

"I guess only a few tablespoons. Not enough to be an entire life, right?"

"Give it the morning and come in if anything seems different. Okay? I'm not worried. You shouldn't be either."

I don't go in and I somehow manage to avoid the news for a few uneventful days, but Mark catches the chaos from the radio while driving into town for supplies. After unloading the groceries, he strokes my belly and furrows his brow.

"What's wrong?"

"A mass event. Something terrible."

I place my hand atop his and wait for Ava to stir.

"Something that affects the womb."

I think of that night. How it felt more like a dream, or a nightmare.

"She's still there. It's okay. I can still feel her there."

"But the blood."

"The doctor said it was fine."

"The thing you saw!"

"Pregnancy brain. Northern lights. I don't know."

"What about Dirt? He won't come near you anymore without hissing."

"So now the cat's a barometer for my well being?"

I pick at the scabbed scratches on the top of his hand as Mark works at prodding my wounds.

"Honey, I love you and I don't want to break your heart, but we need to check under the hood. We need another ultrasound."

I keep to myself that my cravings have changed. I want meat. I can smell and hear everything. Things are just different. The cat is right, but I'm not ready to say goodbye to Ava. Or hello to whatever has taken her place.

The next day, by some miracle of scheduling, the gynecologist braces us for bad news. She offers us a grief counselor before she even turns on the imaging machine. I don't speak. Mark leads the interrogation.

"So?"

"It's exactly like the others. I'm sorry."

"How does a child disappear? Where does an entire baby go?"

"There is something here. It's just not her. She's been replaced."

"By what?"

"I can't be certain, but it's doglike. Four legs, a tail. I'm sure you've been watching the news."

"A dog?"

"I'm not an animal doctor, by any means. But the structure looks canine."

"So it's not Ava anymore?"

"It's clearly something else. I'm sorry."

"Makes sense now, why Dirt won't come near you. You're harboring the enemy of his people."

"I'm going to step out and leave you two to process this. Take all the time you need."

She doesn't mean the last part, because after ten minutes we're being asked to give the room up for the next devastated couple.

Most of the drive home is quiet. The ultrasound picture, a sad party gift, a tragic consolation prize, has fallen between the seat and the door. I make no moves to retrieve it from that place of other dropped and nearly forgotten things. It makes a permanent home there beside a stale french fry, a long missing earring, and my hopes and dreams. Maybe if we'd conceived earlier the wave would have missed us and we'd be the one house standing after the tsunami. We could be safe inside with our son or our daughter, braiding hair or playing with cars. Holding them close while watching expectant mothers all around us panic over the growing issue of just what was growing inside them. I snap at the thought of the alien I'm transporting.

"I want it out of me! I don't want anything to do with it anymore!"

I go for my buckle and think of opening the truck door.

"This isn't the end, babe. Things will just be different," says Mark, the eater of the bruised banana, the scraper of the blackened layer of burnt toast, the acceptor of all things in their lesser forms.

"I don't want things to be different! I want toast that isn't burned to begin with!"

"What?"

"Never mind."

My trees bend. Mark is the wind.

We wait in the Returns line to get back our money for the crib. Other pregnant women bid farewell to their dreams as they hand over receipts for changing tables, diaper genies, and mobiles. Sale signs hang from the ceiling and red clearance stickers cling to everything. It seems a bit preemptive, to close an entire industry centered around the future arrival of human infants. Maybe things will go back to how they were some day. They could make this a storage facility until then. And if we never see normal again, then a museum of days gone by. The woman in front of me chats on her phone in some kind of strange, blissful, modern resignation.

"I'm keeping the baby clothes. I've seen people online who dress up their dogs in onesies so I'm thinking I can use it all anyway. Maybe open an IG account. I don't even have receipts for most of it."

Just another day at the end of the world.

We're nearly to the front of the line when something happens to all of us who are expecting. We fall to the floor in unison as our parasites shift aggressively in our bellies, an intelligent, coordinated movement that feels like they're trying to run in a herd. We moan and cry in symphony until the moment passes.

The cashier avoids eye contact. I can't take it personally. She's a witness to a war, a minimum wage civilian casualty who returns me without question my money for a crib that we couldn't fit back into its box.

"I think it's missing screws."

She shrugs. "We all are."

I stare at the empty space against the wall where the crib used to be. It stares back at me. I turn my gaze to the window and the fields beyond it. How I ever thought anything could grow here, I don't know. It's all dead. The meat cravings worsen. The movements from inside my womb become violent, predatory, pushing boundaries and testing my strength. I begin fighting back. I stop eating, deny it sustenance. It chews at the walls of its holding cell. I eat sushi everyday and only myself end up sick. I drink cases of wine and hit Mark in fits of drunken anger. Nothing I'm willing to do will kill it. Life keeps finding a fucking way. Our marriage suffers. The health of the

womb persists.

"You're not well," Mark says to me one night in the dark of the hallway after I've vomited in the toilet.

"Good. If I'm not well, it means he's not well."

Mark slaps my face. I tussle with him, hoping he punches me in the stomach, begging him to push me down the stairs. I hadn't conjured the strength to do it myself. He throws me against the wall, forcing more bile up my throat and onto his shirt.

"Goddamnit, you smell like an alleyway!"

"I'm grieving, Mark."

"This isn't grief, this is murder! It's suicide! We lost Ava. I'm not going to lose you too!"

"What am I supposed to do?"

"Learn to fucking love it until we have a better option!"

Third Trimester - "I hate you soooo much! I do, I do!" This from my mouth in a singsong voice that Mark hates. Mark with splinters in his hands from building a dog run in the backyard with the wood leftover from reinforcing the fence. Mark with back pain from tearing up the plush carpeting of the nursery in order to lay easy-to-clean linoleum. Mark with apparent budding love for this thing that's begun clawing to get out of me.

"Why are you spending all this energy? And money?"

"Don't you think we should pretend to be excited? Nurture the damn monster?"

"I can cease my attempts at fetal murder to protect you, but it's not in me to read picture books about humans to an alien lifeform feeding off my body."

"I mean, think of what it'll do to us when we don't

coo over it! I don't want it for one second to suspect that we aren't eagerly awaiting its arrival."

Mark is right, though I hate the idea. Loving it seems like dishonoring Ava's life and ignoring what could have been. Maybe a bit of her spirit will live on in the creature that consumed her. I survey the mound for signs of life and it wiggles inside me. I fear it can read my thoughts.

"I don't want you, but you're what I've got," I say in the direction of my navel.

I pull the baby name books from the boxes in the closet and pore through them for anything fitting of the abomination in my gut. Hundreds of pages, thousands of names, and not one suitable moniker for the beast. I am a woman possessed by an unnameable thing, inhabited in utero by a demon holding onto its power through resolute anonymity. I see a name near the end of the alphabet and it gives me an idea.

"You're what I've got, Russ."

"Russ, huh?" Mark asks from the doorway. "Short for Russell?"

"Short for Cerberus."

He laughs until he sees I'm serious.

"It's not three-headed."

"No, but it might as well be. And it's doglike. Besides, the name means flesh-devouring, which fits since it ate our unborn daughter. It ticks all the boxes."

"Are you drinking again?"

"No, I'm having a moment of clarity. Or at least a little fun."

Every night of the final week of my pregnancy, I slip out

of bed and the house and slither under it, into the crawl space and beneath the room with the water heater, a pocket of warmth against the bitter twilight. Something about the smell of the dirt there calls to the thing inside of me, like it knows the Earth will eventually be his. New territory for his species, a next claim, maybe a final conquest. I can't ignore the draw. Mark spends the first few nights in a camp chair outside, but gives up his watch when he loses feeling in his toes.

The Birth - I wake to cobwebs on my face as the early morning light finds the vent openings of the crawl space. I remember the low ceiling and sit up part way to transition to all fours. It feels good to allow my giant belly to hang. The thing inside of it rolls to get comfortable in a new position and wetness runs down my legs. A cramp pulls me down.

"Mark!" I scream as loud as I can, willing my call for help through the foundation and into a cracked window, up through the floorboards and into his ears.

I crawl to the small opening. Dirt greets me, hissing, hackles raised, attempting to keep Russ and I in the dungeon where we belong.

"Get out of here!" Mark snaps at the cat, who slinks off with a look back that suggests Mark too should walk away while he can.

"My water."

"The baby's coming?"

"Don't call him that."

"What should I call him? Russ, the three-headed, the child devourer, the bastard son of our new alien overlords?"

"Just take me to the hospital!"

Mark pushes the boundaries of spacetime as he speeds down the gravel lane toward the highway. Maybe we'll get lucky and the truck will hydroplane, lift off, and take Russ back to the stars. Maybe we'll get luckier and travel back in time to avoid the whole thing. There aren't any street lamps this far out, but a car passes on occasion, its headlights illuminating the pale upholstery of the truck's cab and sending an arch of light across the dome of my belly, like watching night chasing day on a globe. The seatbelt crosses that same surface, gently resting on the biggest part of my abdomen. Russ knows it's there and scratches along the inside of my womb, tracing the edges of the strap.

I imagined this differently, with Mark looking over at me lovingly as I labor in the passenger seat, with joy taking hold and displacing any fears we might have. His eyes are on the road though and he's somewhere else entirely. I'm in the darkness of the fields as the frost works at covering them. How I'd like the blanket of that long, cold nap.

"Almost there. Are you doing okay?" He snaps me from my dying daydream.

"I'm scared. I'm not ready to meet him."

"Don't worry. It'll be just like adopting a dog."

"Yeah. The one thing I didn't want to do."

Vehicles clog the parking lot of the hospital. Sedans, ambulances, news vans, animal control units. Bulbous, grimacing, dirt-covered women limp and waddle through the vestibule like penguins as their partners fight to stay close to them in the shuffle. Mark and I join the flow and let it pull us inward. Between the sets of sliding doors we're confronted by our own bizarre perfume and we gag on that mix of soil and fear, blood and amniotic fluid. Once again the proximity of our wombs throws us into a choreographed lurch, which spills us into the lobby.

"No! No beds!" Someone yells from an interior hall. The mob surges forward again, displaced by the size and severity of that information.

"We're overwhelmed! Over seventy women are in labor here!" the front desk woman barks.

"But he's coming!" I bellow, somehow having made it to the front of the rookery. "He's coming!" The pain of another contraction pushes the words from my throat, transforming me into a terrified summoner of a devil slowly rising from the center of the pentagram I never meant to draw on the floor.

"If I had a dollar for how many times I've had someone scream that in my face tonight, I'd be raiding the vending machine instead of sitting here putting up with this shit!"

Mark pulls my arm to lead me away from this fight he thinks I'll pick, but the receptionist is another innocent civilian, shell shocked by the sight of an invasion. At minimum, she deserves Cheetos.

I spot a wheelchair left unattended outside a bathroom door. Neither of us worry about who we've stranded inside. Mark parks me down a hall next to another woman in a similar state as mine. My right arm dangles over the edge of the armrest and the woman gives my hand a squeeze.

"It's my f-f-first." Her weak voice breaks as she enters another contraction of her own. A name tag, stuck to her chest and crinkling as she writhes, reads 'Rachel'.

I don't know if she means her first child, or her first live birth of an alien being. Ripples and mounds move beneath her shirt, claws form tiny peaks as they push toward the surface.

"I feel like I'm dying."

"You aren't dying, Rachel. It's going to be okay." I'm grateful for her as a distraction from my own predicament.

She's gritting her teeth as discs of blood bloom and expand on the cotton landscape. "They told me it would hurt."

"This is normal then, this is normal. Breathe through it."

I rest a hand on her belly, applying gentle pressure to slow the bleeding. I look for Mark, he's down the hall hailing passing medical staff like taxis, but no one wants his fare. My hand is wet.

"She needs a doctor!" The taxis continue to fly by. The Lamaze breathing is a home med kit Band-Aid clinging to the wet, bulging edges of a complete evisceration. Her breathing falls behind. It might be making it worse, the expansion pushing everything up and away like geysers. I place my other hand where it looks the most red as I try to think back to birthing class, to the part of the course where they prepare you for bleeding out through your abdomen. It must have been the week Mark and I had to skip because of car trouble.

"Breathe. Remember what they taught us." I breathe with her, trying to calm myself with every exhalation, wishing I could forget all of this. Her breathing changes pattern, a sputtering engine losing steam before stopping altogether. I can feel the claws on my palms. Her beast child makes its final moves to break out of its shell where it ends up tangled in her bloodied shirt. My hands slip on the grips of the wheelchair. I can't roll away, stuck at the scene of the crime thinking of ways to explain the blood on my hands.

"It's crawling out of her!" I scream to the passers by, but they are tending to their own chest-bursters. I wet myself, my bladder no match for the combination of terror and tensing as a contraction rocks me. Suddenly my wheelchair is moving away from the dead girl, merging into the traffic of the hall.

"Good news, you've skipped the line," the pusher says, "that girl with the exit wound was next."

I look behind us and see Mark rushing to catch up.

A doctor turns us away from the birthing suite. "Not this room, the operating room! She needs a c-section! They all need c-sections!"

"I don't want a c-section. That wasn't part of the plan."

They already have me on a table.

"Listen, you're going to end up with a cesarean either way. That mini Freddie Krueger you've finished brewing under your nightgown will make shredded beef of your insides if you don't let me cut you open with this scalpel. Your choice."

"Mark, tell them I don't want a c-section."

"Babe, none of this is to plan. It's okay. Let them do their work."

Mark's no longer eating bruised bananas, he's making full on banana bread compromises.

I can feel the sharp needles pressing upward toward the bright light of the medical lamp. I close my eyes and I'm transported to that night in the nursery. The spaceship is above the field. A beam penetrates my womb, illuminating it like a sphere of amber, our hellhound the bug within.

"I don't like the look of it!" I scream as something touches my legs. I expect to see Dirt there, circling, but I'm back at the hospital where the surgeon is fussing with the stirrups.

"The look of what? Don't worry! This is perfectly normal!" He assures me as he dons thick leather gloves, which nearly meet his shoulders.

"But I'm having a dog, Doctor, not a falcon."

The labor team releases nervous, pre-show laughter. I make a mental note regarding my deathbed hilarity. It's a shame you only die once.

"Remember that for the funeral, Mark. The falcon joke. For the eulogy."

"Shhh, honey. Don't say things like that. You aren't dying."

"That's what I told the girl in the hall, but she was. Look."

I lift my still bloody hands to show him as the invader is tugged from my body and for a few brief moments, I feel free again. Mark cuts the umbilical cord and skips the opportunity to stab the thing to death.

Russ struggles in the nurse's arms, a dog not yet trained to be held. I wish the whiplash from the sudden snap back to reality would have killed me. I could do with a broken neck right about now.

"Congratulations! He's beautiful!" The words, a habit from decades of running the maternity ward, fall out of the doctor's mouth before he can catch them. I'm too stunned to argue.

Russ and I stare at each other with wild eyes of the same shade of blue. It's the only resemblance I can see.

His skin is black and scaly, with small tufts of randomly distributed fur poking out. His tail shrinks and grows at will. His face and shape is doglike, but in an off way, like a child's drawing come to life. I don't like the look of it at all.

"I don't think you're the father, Mark."

It gets a morose chuckle out of him. The nurse smiles. The doctor wisely opts for silence.

"What's his name?" the nurse asks.

"Russ," Mark offers.

"Ah, a popular name lately."

My ego deflates like my womb. I'm not even as clever as I thought.

"Would you like to hold him?"

"No," we reply in unison.

"Okay, then we're going to kennel him and close you up. And then maybe we can find you a room."

I lie on the operating table and mistake the glow of the lamp for sunlight. The urge to leave overwhelms me. Mark leans in for my whisper.

"How much time do you think we have until he chews through the metal?"

"I don't know, but as soon as they wheel you out of this room, we're making a break for it."

Mark and I escape shortly thereafter. He pushes me in the same soiled wheelchair from before the birth. We squint against the sunlight and find a way through the battlefield of the front lawn of the hospital. Bodies of women, torn to pieces, make it a difficult path. Russ whines and barks behind us, already free of his cage. He reaches the truck as we pull away.

"Drive! Drive!"

A small pang pulls the walls of my heart together as I watch Russ chase the car in the rearview mirror. How desperately he wants to be near us, how fervently he nips at our heels.

We break away from the repetitive blocks of the city into the calmer suburbs and finally back to the fields of the North. Somewhere behind us, Russ runs without rest. Mark slows the truck to a more acceptable speed. My abdominal incision aches and leaks blood through my shirt, a red, frowning mouth above my groin, echoing my sentiment on the whole absurd affair.

An hour after we arrive home, Russ bursts through the doggie door, his internal homing beacon more accurate than the truck's GPS system. He finds me on the couch where I'm resting, wraps his elongated tail around my neck until I'm gasping for breath, and tears through my shirt to nurse. It's a relief at first for my milk-filled breasts, until he begins to gnaw. I tell him 'no' as forcefully as I have the energy to and he lets up enough for me to not fear my life. I lose as much blood as milk and pass out from the trauma. I dream of leaving him on the steps of a far away church or at the edge of the yard in a cardboard box emblazoned in black marker 'FREE TO A GOOD OR BAD HOME'.

Days later, Dirt disappears as suddenly as he showed up so many months ago. Eventually I find his collar bloodstained and abandoned in the front yard. I bend to pick it up and Russ drops a bone at my feet, something scavenged from the farmland around us. It's human. A temporal bone. Less a gift, more a warning. Mark takes it from me and flings it across the yard like a Frisbee for Russ to bring back. They play tug-of-war.

"Really? Aren't you concerned?"

"He probably found a graveyard!"

"It'll be your skull soon!"

I abandon them in the yard and cry as I throw Dirt's collar and any lingering bits of optimism into the trash. It's all caution now. All I wanted was that cat and Ava and that picture window. I didn't expect this.

Postpartum - I train myself to get out of bed every day despite the depression. I train Russ to sit. Mark trains himself how to shoot the gun he's purchased by turning the spruces into the receiving end of a range, but then he reads online that the beast child's skin is bulletproof and boxes up the firearm for good and starts taking Russ on walks.

Russ runs circles around me when he's hungry, keeping me from anything other than feeding him. When he herds Mark and I together, he wants us to mate, threatening us with his elongated tail until we're in the act, choking Mark if he loses his erection too soon. It's hard to be turned on when we're forced into sexual servitude for the procreation of an alien race.

We scrub shit and saliva off the baby pink walls of the nursery and we settle into our bizarre routine of demented domesticity. My motherly masquerade and Mark's fatherly farce both sweeping brush strokes in our discount American Gothic.

The stitches in my abdomen haven't even dissolved before I am again pregnant. Russ knows before anyone. We waste no money on a test. It's confirmation enough the way he stares up at my belly, the noises he makes at the new life inside me, and eventually, the howling calling back from within.

Once more my womb expands and I feel the urge to return to the dirt beneath the farmhouse to rest. Russ sleeps beside me, guarding the life in me which belongs more to him than Mark or I. In the house above, in another world, Mark reads late into the night, pouring through speculation on the alien's Achilles' heel, searching for ways to kill Russ before the wandering strays and boneyards no longer satisfy his growing hunger, before the twins arrive and we are outnumbered, before the beings who placed this plague upon us land for the final invasion.

"ONE NEED NOT BE A CHAMBER TO BE HAUNTED; ONE NEED NOT BE A HOUSE; THE BRAIN HAS CORRIDORS SURPASSING MATERIAL PLACE."
-EMILY DICKINSON

THE BUG HOUSE

Back then, all the older kids claimed they'd made it a night in The Bug House and they'd hang it over our heads that we hadn't. They called it a "rite of passage", which meant nothing to Danny or me at the time, but they sure made it sound like something we should care about. Our parents told us to stay away from it and, even now, my mother begs me to leave the bad memories buried. But thirty years is a long time to be haunted by a place and a person, to fear killing a spider out of thinking it'll have its revenge. From the day my family and I moved away, I'd been trying to convince myself that The Bug House didn't exist and that Danny had the same chance I did to grow up and grow old. Countless hours and entire paychecks spent on therapy, all these decades between me and the madness, yet I was unable to save my marriage from a phantom, incapable of stopping the nightmares. Returning to that address is my one remaining option. Maybe that's what Danny's spirit has been trying to do all these years, pull me back to confront the past and that godforsaken two-story.

Once in town, I look for the farmhouse in my car, but the turns don't reveal themselves and somehow I end up lost in the suburban maze. I wouldn't be surprised to discover that the house sprouted six legs of its own and changed location, or even that the bugs had joined forces to uproot and transfer their building to another spot. But really, things have changed in many normal, small ways—news streets, new signals, new paint—it's all added up to be just enough to confuse me. If I'm to solve this labyrinth, I need to start at the beginning, the house I grew up in.

As kids, Danny and I must have taken our bikes down this sloping driveway and across town to The Bug House damn near a hundred times, trying to work up the guts to go inside. My bike is long gone, but an old two speed rests against the neighboring house. No chains or locks, no expectation that anyone in this town might ride off on this combination loot and getaway vehicle. I pull it away from the siding, breaking the weeds and webs grown up around the forgotten chariot. I feel a pang of guilt that if discovered to be missing, this bike and its new and solemn expedition might alter the owner's view of the neighborhood, might compel them to decline a future gifted casserole out of mistrust, might have them locking an up-until-this-point-never-locked front door. But my crime is a temporary act and not a sign of a coming trend so I think to leave a note, one Danny and I could have written as kids. *Gone to The Bug House. See u later.* All our 'e's as backward as our decisions and, being written in pen, just as unfixable and permanent. But it's best to not mention The Bug House, taboo as it is. I scribble something else on the back of a receipt, something simple, brief, and with a touch of my Midwestern good manners—*Borrowed, not stolen. Sorry!*—and set it in one of the ruts left by the tires.

I smile when I see the tires aren't flat and no rust grips the chain. I kick off and the memory kicks in, muscle and otherwise. I'm ten again, racing Danny down the streets, grateful he's always been faster than me and it's only the back of his now eyeless head I can see.

When we find the lot, The Bug House still stands, grey and ominous, crumbling, but imperishable behind its fence. Just as ageless as the hum of its inhabitants, that thrum not a day older or any different than when I heard it last, some three decades ago. I've always thought this place could outlive everything, including the town that's shunned it.

"Do ya think they'll ever tear it down?" Danny asks from his post beside me, unfazed that I now tower over him because I grew up and he didn't.

"No, I don't think so," I tell him, keeping my eyes forward on slightly less frightening things than my dead best friend.

"Because of what the older kids say?" he continues.

I rack my brain for what it was they'd said. Some lie to scare us. That if the house came down the bugs would come spilling out, a flood of wings and legs moving toward town, a Hokusai-esque great wave of creepy crawlies cresting then crashing down upon us younger kids, and bent on overtaking us specifically, because the bugs knew we couldn't get away as fast. Even now, the thought of it makes me want The Bug House to stay standing until I'm dead, until I'm under the ground and only have the worms to worry about.

"It's not the town's to tear down." I hadn't said that to him back then, but I could now, now that I was older and I'd done a bit of research. "The deed's missing."

I feel him looking at me, probably because he doesn't know what a deed is or maybe because he knows I've strayed from the script of the past.

Even with the deed, I doubt anyone wanted to claim ownership of the house, not with all it's vermin and decay and definitely not after what happened here. If the place belongs to anyone, it's Danny, who never got to leave it, inheriting it when he became as permanent as the bugs.

I worry for a moment that someone will drive by and see me here and call the Sheriff, who'll come ask me why I'm having a staring contest with their moldering architecture, who may recognize me from the day I traded him Danny in one bag so he could put him in another. But hardly anyone ever comes out this way unless they're leaving town and don't plan on looking back. "It's not where the town begins," all the adults here like to say, "it's where it ends." They'd made sure of that. Sometime before our encounter with the house and the bugs, the local council voted unanimously to move the edge of town to the other side of the parcel, effectively abandoning it to the farmland. Condemned in all ways, but a sign on the door.

Danny's still looking at me, waiting, and where he had no eyes, I can see more and more appearing and erupting like blemishes on the skin of his puffy face until he has too many and no matter where I turn I can't feel unseen. He's been one-upping himself for years with these monstrous transformations, each one more terrifying than the last. I should be scared, but it's still him.

"The bugs don't know where we live." I say it to

satisfy his attachment to that day, the last one of his life, hoping he'll look away again and stop silently asking me to gaze into the reproducing peepers in his face. I've been replaying these moments in my head for so long, all the energy and emotion, save for utter fear, have drained from the words. I pray he doesn't notice the uneasiness and lack of conviction in my recited lines. If he can grow eyes, he could produce fangs.

He shrugs. "They *could* probably find us if they wanted."

I think now of the chemical trail of two pre-pubescent boys. The sweat from our hands on the rocks and sticks, from our testicles and onto the pavement as we sat on the hot summer sidewalk. We were everywhere we touched. "They could probably find us if they wanted." I repeat his words and Danny's body hums and vibrates in insectile response. I can feel it through the concrete, climbing my legs. I'm not sure if the communication is good or bad, but his extra eyes heal up and he's left blind again, which I suppose is a bit of both.

I'm so entranced by the house and Danny's bizarre physical communion with the bugs that it takes me some time to realize I'm still gasping for air from the ride here. I set the bike down on the sidewalk, its handlebar resting on harmless chalk butterflies and bumblebees, once brilliant neons, now faded, rain-washed, and approaching indecipherable; another generation's naive depictions of what they think might flutter beyond the walls of The Bug House, a wholly inaccurate rendition of my adversaries.

"These are *nice* bugs," Danny's voice says, but he's disappeared and his voice sounds muffled as though it's tucked away beneath layers of fabric and batting.

"Nothing like those nasty bugs inside, huh?" I nearly yell it because I'm not sure how far away Danny is now.

"Who are you talking to?"

I jump to my feet at the sound of another voice. A girl no older than eight, with blonde pigtails and pink chalk-covered hands, stands next to me on the sidewalk.

"Just a friend. I was talking to a friend, but he...he ran off somewhere." I feign looking around, but I'm too terrified I'll find him and his empty sockets boring into me for falling off the tracks of our storyline again. Satisfied with my explanation, she crouches down close to the chalk on the concrete and points at the butterfly.

"I drew that one! Actually I drew all of 'em, but I like that one the most."

I coo briefly over her art, enough to encourage her future endeavors and to avoid giving her a complex about what are actually mediocre drawings, but all I can think is if I don't get her away from The Bug House, it'll keep her. She won't have a future as a subpar artist, she won't have a future at all. She's not my kid to tell to go home, but thankfully a woman calls out a name I can't decipher and a "time for dinner" and the little girl skips away, oblivious to how close she stood to a possible premature end.

When my breath finally returns to normal, I turn back to the task and approach the fence surrounding the house. It quivers and I look to my left to find Danny back, sticks in hands, twirling up the silken spider's webs like cotton candy from between the diamond mesh. The arachnids scramble for safety. One makes it up a stick, Danny's arm, and then his neck, climbing until it reaches the darkness of one of his orbital caves, where it seeks refuge in the black. I shiver when Danny doesn't blink, because he can't.

I remember when we both were young, how we'd made a game of clearing out the spiders from the city they'd made and feeling that childish sense of accomplishment we granted ourselves over a job well done, even if it was a job no one asked us to do. And just like Danny and I, they'd all return by the next day, their tiny legs having worked overnight to rebuild what we destroyed, binding the weave of the metal grid tighter with each finished web, thereby reinforcing the strength of the fence and the dominion of the bugs. I don't see any sticks, so I leave the work to Danny, who's giggling in his forever-young voice at the devastation he's enacting, so lost in that joy he doesn't notice I'm not helping.

"Get the rocks!" he finally yells, a field commander heading into battle, demanding grenade support to attack our enemies further afield in the grass.

I use the toe of my shoe to feel around for a stone, but everything is so overgrown, I have trouble finding any of the pebbles gathered where the sidewalk meets the lot. He wants me to throw them into that jungle, but I'm not sure I'm ready to revive anything buried there. We'd tossed so many rocks over the fence when we were kids, the lawn would be a field of landmines for the blades if anyone cared to mow it. We were invaders, poking and prodding and asking for some kind of response from the place. I can't blame the house for wanting to take a little bit of what was ours.

Thinking it might be easier with my hands, I squat and feel around beneath the small gap under the gate in the fence. My fingers find the coolness of a large, smooth stone, half buried in the dirt. It's much larger than what we'd normally throw, capable of taking out a window if I chucked it hard enough with my adult arms and I do think of launching it toward a pane. I'd like to hurt the house, but thinking of a hole in the glass feels less like a victory blow and more like disturbing a hornets' nest.

Danny doesn't say anything, but I feel him growing impatient, as though me missing the rock throwing battle could cost us the entire war. I finger dirt away from the edges of the stone, but it's so big, I can't get it out of the ground without moving the gate. I need this rock for Danny. I didn't come here to relive that day, but I can play and if it's what Danny wants, it's the least I can do for him.

He's standing over me now, his tiny frame casting an impossibly sized shadow onto the yard and the house. The shadow grows larger by the second, wiggling back and forth as it rises, sprouting excess limbs in silhouette until he's a centipede with the head of a boy.

"I'm trying!" I screech at the thing as I reach up, lift the latch on the gate, and push it open just enough to give headroom for the rock. With the gate and grass out of the way, I raise it from the ground and see it for what it really is. The engraved script on the memorial stone reads 'Danny'.

Shadow Danny falls like a dropped towel as the stone slips from my hands and I collapse backward onto my butt on the sidewalk.

"De yuh tosh it?"

That voice again.

"What?" I look to my right to see the little girl, a red sauce of some kind smeared on her lips and cheeks. She's still chewing whatever was for dinner. At first I think she means the rock and I try to find the words to explain that

I didn't mean to disturb this grave of sorts, but then she elaborates—as much as she can anyway—with a mouth full of food.

"If yuh tosh da gay yuh haf ta go insigh."

Even garbled, I recognize every single word. My heart pounds harder than it did from the ride here. It hasn't triggered me to see a ghost. I've been seeing Danny since the day he died. No, I'm used to him now, but those words. The rules. I haven't heard them since that day.

"If you touch the gate, you have to go inside." A familiar male voice repeats low, menacing, and clear.

"Fuck," I hiss as I get up from the concrete and wipe the chalk from my hands. I turn and sure enough, Brad's there in the street behind me, leaning against his Camaro while the engine idles. The muscle car is as new as the day it left the lot and Brad appears just as youthful. The gel in his perfectly coiffed hair catches the fading light of the day, making him appear angelic, which couldn't be further from the truth. I wanted to be ready for him this time, but he showed up without warning, just like he did three decades ago.

"You know it's your fault?" I scream, pointing a pink-chalked finger. "We wouldn't have gone in if you hadn't been such an asshole."

Brad doesn't reply, he doesn't know how to. He's a movie on pause or a nerve-rattled thespian waiting for the right prompt to remember his forgotten lines. Once again I feel Danny's growing rage that I've strayed from the plot. I remember the little girl and find her still standing to my side, her hands over her ears.

"What's wrong?"

"Mommy says I have to cover my ears when I hear

bad words so they don't get inside my head."

"You should go home. This is only going to get worse." I can't think of what else to tell her, or how to explain what I'm seeing that she can't, that things more horrible than bad words will get inside her head, that she'll end up bug-filled like Danny, if she doesn't leave now. Before I can make sure she's gone, Danny resumes the scenario.

"Whose rule?" he challenges Brad, one hand resting on the gate, the other pointing a cobweb-covered stick at the boy seven years our senior. A spider clings to the end of the wood, likely panicking over its separation from its home and hunting ground. I commiserate with it as I shift nervously from one foot to another, feeling like prey caught in a trap.

Brad laughs and smacks a hand on the roof of the Camaro. "Anybody who ever grew up here, you know that!"

Another boy, Martin, climbs out of the car. "Remember," he calls out to us, "if you go inside you have to stay the night."

We'd heard the rules, reminded one another of them every time either of us had been tempted to touch the gate, and as much as The Bug House fascinated us, we weren't curious enough to be stuck inside.

"I didn't mean to touch it." I really didn't, but it was a sorry excuse and something similar to what I'd said the first time it happened when I was ten. Even today, at forty, a full-grown man, I want nothing more than to not go inside the house. "I didn't come to stay the night," I mumble, unprepared to relive this event in its entirety.

"We don't even have our sleeping bags!" Danny pleads before beginning to spin silk for a cocoon, a trick he's learned in the interim and one his apparition has shown me before.

I know what comes next and I don't want it. Maybe if I keep my arms closed, it'll ricochet off of me and this bad trip into the past will end. "Not now, not now, not now," I say, a mantra of denial, but it slams against my chest regardless, the memory of the sleeping bag Martin kept in the trunk of Brad's car, that seemingly harmless bundle chucked at me from the street. The reek of stale beer and old cigarettes wafts up my nose as clear as the day it first did.

"You two can share it!" Brad laughs.

"I want that back in the morning!" Martin yells. "Don't piss in it!"

Danny and I stare, waiting for the punch line of the horrible joke, but the older kids stare back, unwavering.

"Go on," Brad urges us, arms crossed like he has all the time in the world, "we'll wait."

"Do you think it's as bad as everyone says?" Danny asks me as we turn to face the house once more, oblivious to the fact that it's about to end his life for the second time.

"Even our parents are scared of this place."

"But not us, right? We aren't scared of anything."

Maybe we should have been, I think. "Let's just get it over with," I say as I step through the opening and into the yard.

Neither Danny nor I stray from the stepping stones leading to the porch. The overgrown lawn twitches and ripples as things move toward us.

"Remember the rest of the rules!" Brad yells from the safety of the other side of the fence.

"We can't kill anything," Danny says to me as leads the way up the decaying front steps to the door.

"And we can't come out until the morning." I turn and look at the sun as it imperceptibly falls to the horizon, clutching the musty sleeping bag like a life vest, knowing what little it will do to keep us safe.

At Danny's urging, I grip the knob, then, now, and push until the front door creaks open. Its rusty hinges announce our arrival.

"Great," Danny says with a sigh. "Dinner is served."

I remember laughing then, but I can't laugh now knowing what happens, not even to please him. I ignore his gaze and step into The Bug House.

The gothic wallpaper hangs more off the walls than on and it's lost its luster, but where it remains I still recognize its paisley pattern in greens and golds. Here and there the lines tremble and move in and out of focus. I don't need to look closer to know it's thousands of small bugs using the curls of the teardrop shapes as mini super highways. It's all moving. Everything writhes.

Straight in front of us a stairway leads to the second floor. I'm grateful to whichever bugs long ago ate away most of the wood. I can't imagine what lives in the bedrooms above our heads. To the right of the stairs, a long hallway runs all the way to the back of the house, but the path is unusable due to the giant funnel web filling the corridor.

"Wow! We'd need a tree's-worth of sticks to clear that thing."

Danny, in awe, reaches out to touch it and I try to grab his hand, terrified of what beast he might summon, but mine falls through his. The spider in his eye socket seizes the opportunity to exit onto more recognizable ground, running down his arm and into the depths of the funnel.

To our right, two termite mounds, as tall as I am,

frame an opening in the wall that leads into the living room. I don't want to enter it, but my night is on rails, and I'm being pulled through these gates to hell. I stand in the center of the space, waiting for Danny to pry his ghostly hand from the funnel web's grip and follow behind me.

Everything I see, the funnel web, the mounds, the bugs on the walls, it's all the same as it was thirty years ago, only bigger, more. Soon, the termite cathedrals will be load-bearing towers, replacing the chewed up walls around them to support the house's center beam. The bugs on the wall will continue walking in paisley shapes even when all the wallpaper falls to the floor. Everything is worse, but maybe this time I can save him, rewrite history and give his spirit and my mind some peace.

"We're going to step on something if we walk around." Already I've been tiptoeing between bugs.

"We don't have to explore," Danny tells me. "Let's just put the sleeping bag down and keep the bugs away until the morning."

I do as Danny suggests and unzip the bag to its full size, creating a rectangular fabric island in the middle of the otherwise bare floor. The bugs stay away from it for a time, its foreign odor and synthetic material repel them, but eventually they investigate, edging closer to the stinking, hemmed polyester.

"If anything comes too close, I'll shoo it away with my stick." Danny holds it like a wand, assigning power to the crooked wood, pretending to zap anything encroaching on our newly claimed territory.

My stomach growls, silently prompted by my knowledge of the story line.

"Sure is good we had pizza earlier." Danny pats his

tummy and I remember the greasy, filling meal we had long ago.

"Yeah," I reply, though his reality isn't mine. I wish I'd thought of eating dinner in town before coming here. I'd give anything for a slice. I'll be starving by morning.

When the sun sits firmly below the horizon, the house wakes to its full squirming splendor. More and more bugs emerge from the holes in the walls and floor, marching in search of food and supplies to fortify their homes and ending up distracted by the curious, four-limbed creatures taking up space in the living room.

Danny covers a yawn so none of the swarming gnats fly into his mouth. "I'm tired."

"You can sleep. I'll keep watch."

He lies down and maybe he closes his eyes, but they don't really work like that anymore. I last a good few hours, blowing away anything that tries to come near, listening to the memory of Danny snoring. The comfort of letting him rest, of being with him again, the long drive, the exertion of the bike ride, and the hum of the bugs combine and, against all of my efforts, lull me to sleep.

Not long after, I'm shaken awake by a frightened Danny and before he speaks, I know the past can't be changed. "Something crawled down my throat," he claims.

"It's a nightmare. Go back to sleep."

"But I feel it inside of me."

I can already see the swelling starting in his lips and cheeks. His breathing changes and I know his throat is closing.

"It hurts." He manages those words as he clutches his

neck.

Water won't help when he can barely breathe, but I leave him there to find a tap. I can't see him like this again, thickened, gasping. I push through a swinging door off the living room and enter into what seems to be a kitchen now transformed into something out of science fiction. Papery nests cascade down from the cabinetry and cling to the sides of the center island. Protected like this in the depths of the house, the wasp nests have grown out of control into one giant community.

I feel around in the near dark, my hands caressing the moonlit, scalloped layers of the nests, until I reach the sink. The pipes groan for a moment and when the sound stops, I expect water to flow, but nothing leaves the faucet.

"Damn it! Why am I here?" I kick the cabinet beneath the sink and the thin wood cracks and splinters. The wasps stir and buzz as the noise of the impact reverberates through the room. I'm surprised Danny doesn't show up in here with wings and a stinger, but he's too busy dying a second death to haunt me from his first.

By the time I find my way back to him, he's quiet, but still alive. Tiny wisps of air escape his swollen lips and in the small beam of light coming in through the window, I can see the slow rise and fall of his chest. If he can hang on until the morning, let his stomach acid kill whatever crawled inside of him, and then sleep the rest of the night away while I protect him, he'll be okay.

I see movement out of the corner of my eye on the big, water-damaged wall across from the front windows and I can't help but look. There, bark lice form moving mosaics on the mildewed surface. Somehow they all understand one another, choreographed like dancers or programmed like drones, moving within millimeters of one another confidently. They skitter into position to recreate horrific mockeries of my face in various expressions of distress. It's as though they've committed to memory every feeling I've had since I came through the front door. I sit in a trance, hypnotized by the grotesque kaleidoscope, completely unaware of the room around me.

When the show ends and the spell is broken, I look down to see I'm covered in cockroaches. Hundreds of tiny legs hold fast to my exposed skin and my clothes as the bodies they're attached to harvest my heat. I scream and they run for cover as something stirs in the other room.

"You won't want to see this," Danny says, emerging from deep inside the hallway's funnel web. He's more spider than boy now, crawling on eight legs toward something stuck and wriggling in the gossamer. "You won't want to see that either." He lifts a spindly leg to point behind me to where the sleeping bag is on the floor.

He's right. I don't want to look. I'm not ready to see him dead like that again.

"Pretending it doesn't exist won't change it. You already tried that. You've always been such a wimp."

"If I look, will you promise to leave me alone? Can you stop showing up everywhere?"

Again Danny points his spider leg, this time in quiet command.

When I do find the strength to turn my head, I see something worse than expected. The green sleeping bag is white with a cartoon cat printed on its top. Where Danny's messy red mop of hair and stick should be, blonde pigtails and a thick piece of pink chalk stick out instead.

I crawl in slow motion until I reach the side of the

bag. The surface rises and falls in an uneven pattern as more than one thing moves beneath the fabric. The cheerful cartoon cat stares up at me. Embroidered under its smiling face is the name 'Harper'. My hand shakes as I pull back the cloth to reveal her face and then her body. Insects hurry away from the scene of their crimes. The girl from the sidewalk lies prone, a few lingering bugs travel her petite landscape, going about their business as though it's normal for a child to be dead here.

"No! No! What happened to her?"

Danny doesn't answer. Harper does, newly emerged from her cloth chrysalis. Her voice comes from one of the walls, where she's an oversized moth camouflaged into the paper. That decorative golden scrawl covers her sickly green wings as though she was reborn stamped in paisley. "Danny said I could play with him all the time, all I had to do was stay the night in The Bug House. We're playing hide and seek. I'm hiding."

I'm unsure whether I should speak to the moth or her body so I look at Danny inside the funnel web. "Danny wouldn't have asked you to come in here." I say through gritted teeth.

The moth flutters upstairs as the bark lice return to their stage on the big wall and take the shape of Harper's tiny face blown up to ten times its size. They move to mimic the opening of her lips as she says "Danny, the house, what's the difference?"

I smack a hand on the floor, encouraging the bark lice and any other bugs nearby to temporarily scurry away, even Danny retreats a little deeper into the funnel. "We were tricked! The house tricked us! I wasn't going to come inside!"

This time her voice comes from a cockroach running by. "It wasn't a trick. You knew the rules and you touched the gate and the rules say if you touch the gate, you have to g-"

"Stop it with that! Just stop it! Why were you here?"

"You aren't going to like the answer."

"I don't like any of this!"

The cockroach wriggles between the lips of her tiny, swollen mouth and, as though her corpse has regained its spirit, it burps and shudders the words, "I touched the gate."

I strike her dead face and the entire house shakes. She belongs to it now, the same as Danny.

"You can't be mad," Danny scoffs. "It's your own fault. You were staring at the bugs on the wall, just like last time. She died the same as me."

I look closer and it's true. Her head and neck are swollen and her hands are at her throat. Something toxic must have crawled inside her mouth. I see movement in her face and think she might still be alive, but instead I find two centipedes shifting and coiling into tighter balls within the cooling warmth of her sockets, her eyes gone the same as Danny's somewhere beneath the floorboards to feed a colony.

I look for the door on the wall where we came in, but the wallpaper is seamless save for the tiny vertical cracks where each sheet meets the next. I pummel the windows with my fists, but they're thick and my hands do nothing but thump against them dully.

"They meant it. We really can't leave!"

"Get comfortable!" Harper giggles from where she's

now stuck in the funnel web, wrapped in a silk cocoon made by Danny's many limbs. Her laughter fills the room, lapping over itself like waves, growing and falling like the buzz of cicadas, amplified by the woven cone holding her prisoner until it merges with the noise of the bugs. "The door will come back in the morning. Danny can wrap you too if you want! It's like a hug!"

"Keep away from me! Both of you!" I back away from the web and the dead children playing in it, through the termite columns and into the living room where I stumble and fall over Harper's body. I stay there next to it for the rest of the night, keeping the bugs off the best I can while she and Danny amuse one another, shapeshifting into new and frightening things. I spit on my hands to clean off the chalk and I keep my back to the bark lice on the wall.

When the sun finally comes through the broken shutters, the bugs recede into cooler, darker corners. For a moment the farmhouse looks normal, just old and abandoned, and I worry that maybe I hallucinated the bugs, but I see their crafted homes, the noise of them plays outside my head, the funnel spider's web still fills the corridor running the length of the house. And even though the spider and the rest of the bugs are out of sight, Harper is still dead, eaten up in all sorts of ways, with more holes in her body than she should have. I zip the sleeping bag around her. It doesn't smell of cigarettes and beer, or any of that other stuff neither Danny nor her will ever get to know. It smells like fabric softener, like youth. The door is once again where I expect to find it, as though it never went anywhere. It opens normally, as though the hinges didn't disappear during the night.

I drag the sleeping bag onto the porch, down the

collapsing stairs, and through the dewy, overgrown grass. The Bug House looms behind me, humming and threatening to call me back before I've even left the yard. On the other side of the fence, Danny and Harper giggle as they spin sticks in the diamonds and have nothing but the worms to worry about.

> *"I HAD SEEN BIRTH AND DEATH BUT HAD
> THOUGHT THEY WERE DIFFERENT."*
> *-T. S. ELIOT*

BUTCHER AND SHAW

Above Ground

Above ground sometimes, if it isn't a good year for the cicadas, you can hear the babies shrieking from their tiny, reenergized lungs. Before you dig them up, you can hear their little voices cutting a path through decaying fabric, boards of pine or mahogany, and six feet or less of newly-packed soil. I don't know how everyone else ignores their bawling. I hear it in my sleep when I'm able to catch it. In my head, through the pillow, and through the floor, haunting my every inhaled breath.

Shaw and I are in a cemetery tucked behind the fields of an old farming community, ready to dig up another. He throws his jacket over the headstone, to veil the name engraved there and continue a tradition of ours: leaving the child unnamed until the work is done and he is presented to the world.

Where Shaw is a workhorse–shovel in hand, feet already on the holy ground of the burial plot, his entire body prepared to desecrate it—I take my time. I smell the air. My shovel leans against a nearby tree.

"I'm coming for you," I say as I press an ear to the dirt to listen to the mournful song of the child. Shaw always laughs at me for this, my need to soothe these motherless things, coddle them before they gain a second chance at life. I can't help but think I would have liked the comfort myself, back when I hadn't yet emerged from the ground.

"He can't hear ya, Butcher! He's got mama rot in his ears!" Shaw's crude words cut the darkness of the night, and expose the cruel reality of the world around us. It's less a place of rest and more a dumping ground for things destined to be forgotten. Throughout the cemetery, the columns of the mausoleums crumble, sending chunks of granite or marble to mix with the wilted flowers lying uncollected on the unkempt grass that slowly wages war on the readability of the headstones. The urns in the columbarium gather dust that's found a way in through the cracks. But he's right, likely with pus-covered pinna the little one can't even hear himself screaming, let alone my promise through almost two yards of dirt to free him from his decrepit, putrescent prison.

With a heavy, goal-oriented hand, Shaw shoves the sharp, metal edge of his shovel into the ground in front of my face. I watch the spikes of grass disappear beneath the blade, only some of them fortunate enough to recover from the point he's making. "Are you gonna help or what?"

I listen a moment longer to be sure of what I'm hearing. It'd be a waste of time and energy if we dug up the wrong site. I hear the cry once more and Shaw's point is taken. I use my own shovel as support to pull myself upright before pressing its blade into the opposite end of the grave.

Everyone thinks the digging is the worst part, but at least the digging is clean. It's better than anything you'll ever reach in a graveyard, better than anything you'll find in a coffin, apart from the babies. I'd dig all the way back down to hell if it meant I could skip the rotting body part of the job. Don't believe anyone who tells you they'd go to all this work, get so close and personal with a corpse just for a pearl necklace or a wedding ring. There's something wrong with folks like that. Robbing from the living would be far easier.

"Come on, stop daydreaming," Shaw whines, already atop the next grave in his mind. "Let's get this done."

As I move the first shovelful of soil, a dreaded feeling passes over me. How deep will we need to dig? How hard will we be forced to push ourselves? Some graves are deeper than six feet. Some mothers are harder to reach. Some babies take more effort than sometimes they feel like they're worth.

Shaw and I have nearly abandoned jobs as the sun rose as we hadn't yet hit wood. We've also found coffins partially exposed by rain or pushed from the earth by underground currents, requiring little effort to fully unearth them. No job is the same and no two graves are alike, but the babies all need saving, that never changes. The Archfiend is expecting them. I move another shovelful of dirt and watch the green of the grass turn to brown as our progress grows.

One Foot
Maybe it's the noise of the digging, but I can no longer

hear the child's cries. Shaw notices the silence as well and stops to rest a moment on the handle of his shovel. He sighs.

"I hate it when they do that."

"Me too."

There's no actual threat. The baby won't die again. Satan will keep it alive with his supernatural life support until we get the infant real air, but the eerie quiet nonetheless inspires speed in me and an outburst from Shaw.

"Hey, speak up!" he yells as he strikes the ground more forcefully with his shovel. The baby cries once more and I'm reminded there's something to be said for occasional brute force. I'm grateful he has it in him to berate the child. I'm too kind to beat it into shape. It's already having a rough go of it and I prefer to let things take their course, often regardless of how much extra time that takes.

With our screaming serenade recommenced, my mind travels back to the other thoughts that creep in as I dig. "How do they come out so perfect in the end? Shouldn't the baby be dead and rotting too?"

Shaw is somewhere else entirely, head down, focused on the task, unreachable by any usual means. I wait for him to draw a breath and ask again, a bit louder. "Why aren't they rotting like their mothers?"

"Why aren't you rotting with yours?" he retorts. "It's not like you to question the master."

"But don't you ever wonder how he keeps them, and us, from withering away?"

"Don't look at me. I can't pretend to understand his powers. I fully expect to fall apart at any moment."

Even with the wails of the thing, with so many feet still to go, the digging seems endless. One foot down it's hard to feel like we'll ever reach the bottom of the grave. Every scoop of dirt removed sees new dirt flowing in from the walls like bailed water flooding back into a boat with a hole in its side. The goal unreachable. No end. No reward. Just digging, with every particle against our efforts, and each strike of the shovel pushing the baby farther from us, in the opposite direction, deeper into their mothers bodies, out through their backs and the coffin lining to the dirt and rocks beneath the grave. Worse to think, the coffin does not exist at all and the child's cry is but a figment of our imaginations, a bodiless voice of a corpseless baby we can never unearth. Maybe this is Hell and we're doomed to dig forever, or at least until we die and rest in the hole we've made.

Two Feet
Eventually we get into a groove and the rhythmic, alternating sounds of our tools hitting the soil makes for a morbid kind of melody that seems to drive Shaw closer to madness. He speeds up or slows down to upset the perfection of the tune. I change my tempo as well, to chase the song and keep it.

"Knock it off!" He throws a bit of dirt my way, sprinkling my face with grit.

Melodic digging or not, about two feet down my arms are on fire, my focus waning, and I get to thinking it'd be nice if the babies could claw their own way out of the ground, one petite handful of dirt at a time. Wriggle their way up like they wriggled their way out of their bearer, a worm on a blind search for nematodes and rotifers or some air-breathing aquatic animal finally coming to the surface for air. If they could even meet us halfway, somewhere soon in this pit and we could all embrace and congratulate one another because, after all, it's never too early to get used to a life of hard work or to be rewarded with a small break from the full task of it.

Immortal, but not immune to weariness, I stop digging and sit on the grass edging of the grave. My biceps scream nearly as loud as the baby beneath us. Shaw reads this as a cue to take a break as well.

"Maybe these children were meant to die."

"Shaw, don't start. I know you'd rather be with a living broad right now instead of sweating with a man in search of a dead woman, but we aren't stopping until the job is done."

"Listen, Butcher, maybe we're upsetting some kind of balance by digging them up."

"Talk a little louder so the boss can hear you!"

Shaw laughs. "He's too busy to listen in on us."

"He needs pure souls. He can't trust those damned to spend eternity with him. They're evil."

"You know for a fact these babies aren't pure. They're born with the original sin of mankind."

"But only that *one* sin. They haven't lived lives yet, they haven't been exposed to all the temptation in the world. He can trust them like he trusts us. So keep digging like he trusts that we will!"

Shaw looks off into the distance, making faces like he's doing mental math to sort out my logic, trying to find a way out of my rational thinking. He looks down at the work ahead of us and concedes.

"Okay, I'll keep digging, but stop trying to make a fucking song out of it!"

Three Feet

Three feet down and we are properly in the grave, half our bodies peeking above ground, entrenched in the battle, tossing shovel after shovel of dirt into the world above. Below waist there's a noticeable temperature change from the moisture in the soil. It does wonders to moderate the heat from the digging. I wonder if we're recognizable from a distance or if we've merely taken the form of gravestones or stone monuments, our movements signed off by observers as subtle tricks of the night.

A fog rolls in, pouring slowly into our trench. I notice other things moving toward us in the cemetery, spectral forms mixing with the mist. They know we're getting closer to another coffin birth and they rush toward us, a tide of tenderness-fueled rage, a surge of harnessed agony.

"Shaw, it's them. The Mob of Every-Mother."

He looks up to see the semi-transparent swarm on approach, coming to gripe and moan about us taking another child. They hold their empty bellies and swaddling blankets, they nurse nothingness and cry in eternal mourning for their missing offspring.

"Would you have taken the job if he'd told you about the ghosts? I sure as hell wouldn't have. They creep me out." Shaw mimics a dramatic, full body shiver as if the willies have physically manifested and attacked him.

"They're pretty harmless."

"You call this harmless?" Shaw lifts an arm and the mist rises with it, stuck like a spider's webbing to his skin. There's a weight to the gossamer that slows us down, like we're moving underwater. Every shovelful requires more effort. Every baby becomes that much harder to reach.

Shaw finds a rock and chucks it at the gathering, as though the spirits will scatter like raccoons, but the stone passes through them and bounces off a tree, doing nothing to dissuade them.

"Just dig," I say to him, though I don't follow my own advice. I scan the crowd of apparitions for my mother, who I sometimes see in the audience.

"It's definitely slower if you don't help," Shaw barks.

I get back to the dirt without catching a glimpse of her face.

Shaw can't ever seem to stay quiet for long with the bawling of the banshees around us.

"You ever wonder why we don't dig up the girls?" he asks. "I mean, how do we know it's a boy?"

"Satan knows all, the same as God, if you believe in *that* guy."

"So why don't we save the girls too? I bet there's a bunch of them stuck in their momma's bellies underneath the grass here."

I stop digging again and think about it for a second, which is long enough to feel my muscles are really beginning to cramp. "Imagine a girl out here in the dark, long hair falling in her eyes, sweat pouring down her front, digging up babies. Undead or not, they've got too much heart for that. Imagine them tearing infants from their mother's wombs. Heck, think about the dirt beneath their nails. This is a man's job and coffin births dig up coffin births. It wouldn't be right to sign a lady up for this without at least checking with her first."

At some point during my long answer, Shaw stopped digging too. He looks up at me and nods, mumbles something about how babies can't answer questions, and slams the blade of the shovel into the dirt again.

Four Feet

"Still haven't found my grave," Shaw says without looking up. He likes to think he owes his entire existence to Satan, that no mortal mother or father were ever involved in his creation and that his inability to locate the marker bearing his name is somehow proof of that infernal, immaculate conception.

"You don't read the graves. It's intentional. You see or *don't* see whatever serves your purpose. We've probably walked by it already."

"That's better than you, the guy who spent years obsessed with finding his plot, who cried when he finally discovered the hole he was pulled from."

"It's a big deal. Ask any other coffin birth. You'll feel it too someday, if you allow yourself."

"Nah, I don't want to feel anything. Satan won't let me live much longer anyway."

He loses me there. He always loses me there, where he's convinced he'll die an early death. We're already ancient. If there wasn't some unholy magic holding us together, we'd be falling apart by now, not much more than bone like the mothers we were pulled from and just as forgotten too. We've already long ago lived beyond the expectancy of mortal men. Digging up the babies promises us that.

"How long will you have to live to keep you from forgetting you'll live forever?"

Shaw shrugs and hocks a loogie into the sky in a pitiful arc that sends it falling back into the dirt at his feet.

I look again at the sobbing souls surrounding us,

beyond the maternal malevolence distorting their faces, and I find her at the front of the pack.

I've been back to our grave on occasion, between jobs, when my still human heart calls. As long as I live, whatever eternity I'm granted for my service, forever I'll be drawn to my name engraved deep into that granite slab. Bits of moss sit growing in the drops of the letters, but the surname, my name, is still visible.

Butcher, it reads. *Wife. Mother.*

It's the only information the rock allows me of the woman who would have given me a childhood aboveground. The grave has lost all signs of the long ago disruption of my unearthing and she must be down to bones now, it's been so long since one of my older brothers removed me from her festering womb.

Had she wanted me before her passing? Before my birth? My mother reaches out for me now, pleading for me to rejoin her in death, answering any question I've ever had about her love.

Five Feet

I'm pulled from my reverie by a thick, sour perfume escaping from an arc of dirt as it passes.

"Grieving layer, we're getting close now," I whisper with funeral-reserved solemnity.

It's always a unique blend, dependent on the deceased and their family and the messages they wanted to leave in their flowers of final farewell. I imagine the original gathering that came to lay the mother and child to rest. Family and friends circled around a hole much like the one we're digging, wet faces, hands gripping overused tissues, mouths reciting overused psalms. One by one they would have stepped forward to throw in flowers with the first dirt of burial.

"Orchids," Shaw identifies one of the blooms.

"For reverence," I recall. My nose catches the next scent. "And lilies."

Shaw scoffs. "Eternal love. How sweet."

I see the last flower before I smell it. A rose petal, blood red with a hint of blackening decay at its edges, separated from its bud, sitting atop the next scoop of dirt to be removed. "Restored innocence."

"We could retire and become florists," Shaw suggests. "What more knowledge could we need other than the ability to identify flowers by scent and sight?"

What a pair we'd make, two death-hardened men building complicated, yet delicate bouquets packed full of meaning for the still living.

"It's a thought, isn't it?"

THUNK. All and any dreams of doing anything but grave robbing vanish with that first dull thud of metal against wood. The sweat cools on our bodies as we pause to bask in the discovery of the crypt we've been seeking.

"Eureka!" Shaw hoots into the night, a miner finally striking a gold vein deep within a mountain, as the Mob of Every-Mother wails in unified anguish over the same revelation.

The Box

You can tell a lot from a box. Firstly, that if one exists, there's money in the lineage. If it's a casket, with four sides, the family is considerably less well off. A six-sided coffin costs more, an added expense in the angles and engineering.

Only the wealthiest are buried in coffins and the baby and mother would have lived a good life if the mother hadn't died. We could stop right now, seeing the tiered, reddish-brown mahogany, like a layered chocolate cake for the taking. We could trace the owner of the plot, locate the father of the child, the husband of the dead woman, and make some real money robbing the estate instead of their burial grounds, but loyalty dies hard. Satan awaits this child and Shaw and I are bound by a sacred duty to deliver it.

The baby screams, hardier than ever, fully embracing its small life, perhaps sensing the weight lifted off the top of its enclosure. I wait for footsteps, the beam of a flashlight, someone demanding answers about his shrill cries in the night, but no watchman comes, no potential curiosity is great enough to investigate a baby's graveyard lamentations. Even I still find it spooky.

I feel around for the crowbar left somewhere topside. My hand finds the cool, dewy metal and I pull it into the grave with me. The trick is to pry as close to the nails as possible. Less work, less banging and more bang for your buck. Shaw pulls a bandana over his nose and lifts off the lid. He hands it to me and I set it next to the dirt pile above before covering my own face with a handkerchief, bracing myself for the smell. It's not an odor to which one ever acclimates.

Here she is as expected, the formerly expectant mother, dressed in finery. Lace and pearls confirm the social status her burial box suggested. She appears petite in the coffin, small in life and further diminished by death. Perhaps too young to be a mother. The labor that was denied her would have ended her life anyway if something else hadn't gotten to her first.

"Madam." I tip an invisible hat to the corpse, and stare at Shaw until he pays her some similar greeting.

We stop for a moment of silence, giving our quiet condolences for what has happened to her and for what we're about to do.

Bodies rot fast here in the warm, moist climate. I hope someday they'll figure out better ways to decelerate the process, but there is comfort in how unrecognizable she's already become. I can't imagine taking a baby from a woman who appears to only be sleeping.

Piles of maggots and two tiny fists, in their efforts to feast and to escape, respectively, raise the fabric of her burial clothes. I pinch the bottom hem of the dress, hold my breath, and lift the final layer of the putrid Russian nesting doll—dirt, lid, dress—to reveal the child at the center of it all.

We've seen all kinds of post-mortem fetal extrusion. Some babies arrive perfectly, as expected, pushed cleanly through and out. Others experience more difficult entries to this world. Sometimes the gasses don't build up enough for a complete exit, escaping instead through another hole in the abdomen. Sometimes even the babies emerge through the weakened flesh of the belly, like breaching whales from a chaotic sea. Those ones get my stomach the worst, like lifting a piece of bread out of French onion soup, all manner of chunks and sloppy bits hanging on, about the same colors too. But this one, his is a partial birth. His legs are still hidden inside his mother's body. A paraplegic, a morbid mermaid with a whole entire human for a tail.

Neither of us like getting our hands this dirty so we take turns removing the babies. I'm grateful it's Shaw's turn tonight because this will take some tugging, the kind that upsets the entire gurgling ecosystem of the woman's decaying body.

"Sure you don't want to get in there, Butcher? Been a long time since you've *really* been between a woman's legs."

I could drop the lid on him, the crowbar, the dirt. "Ha. Ha. Fuck you."

Shaw squats down at the end of the coffin and reaches forward, gripping around the small chest of the boy.

"Now I've got an idea. If you jump on her chest from up abov-"

"Shaw, no. Stop fucking around and get him out of there."

"You're no fun, Butcher."

"I'm plenty of fun. This just isn't it. We have a job to do."

"There's not a thing written down about how we're supposed to do it though!"

Even if there was some code of ethics, I doubt Shaw would regard it with anything other than contempt.

He pulls on the child, wiggling and twisting him like a wine cork out of the bottleneck. He comes free, but not alone. Things follow after him, pouring out like river water from a burst dam. His mother's abdomen, the roof of a derelict house, collapses after losing the final support of his solid presence.

Lifted above his old home, the boy kicks his freed legs, flinging clumps of decomposing matter in all directions. It sticks to our bodies and mixes with the sweat of our hard work and the dirt already clinging there. Steam thick with the scent of death rises off his slimy body.

"There he is!" Shaw coos, the unspoken duty of an adult holding an infant. Shaw's not actually excited to see the child. He's spent too much time staring at the dirt, moaning in regret about the deal he keeps with the devil, but he loves his immortality more than he hates the job. I've heard him revel just as much as remorse.

The umbilical cord dangles from the baby's belly. Shaw gives the opposite end a tug, bringing the degraded placenta into view, a grey, veined pancake hanging sadly like a deflated balloon.

"You know some people eat this thing?" Shaw pretends to nibble on an edge of the fleshy disc before raising it in offering.

"It's not for me." I pull myself above ground and Shaw hands the baby to me, before he too finds his way to the grass.

"Hello, son of the ground," I say to my new brother struggling in my hold, threatening to slip from my hands and back into the mess he's been born from. "Satan will be pleased. You're a strong one."

"Welcome to the team," Shaw says as he steps behind the grave marker and places his hands on his jacket, preparing to reveal the child's name. With a dramatic lift and toss, the denim is removed and the stone read aloud. "Hughes? Sounds more like a butler than an immortal servant to the dark lord."

"It is a *very* serious name for a baby, but we don't have a choice. We're bound by the markings on the stone. It's why you're Butcher and why I'm Shaw."

"Yeah, yeah. He must maintain a small bit of his humanity. His last name ties him to the world. We don't know what his mother would have called him. Blah, blah,

blah," Shaw prattles.

"As important as his name, does the boy have all his parts?" I count Hughes' tiny fingers and toes. He calms in my arms, comforted by my less clinical touch and finally adjusting to the cool of the evening. "All his digits, fit to dig."

His mother's name is engraved on the marker as well. *Tamara.* He'll never know her and he might never stumble upon his grave here to acquaint himself. Perhaps he'll get lucky like I did.

"Come to collect the kid, have you?" Shaw calls across the cemetery to a new being who moves in the night. Neither of us feel any fear toward the creature as its familiar, slinking shape draws near. We watch her walk the lawn, weaving expertly between the tombstones, her bare skin a dark crimson, just a shade above Satan himself. The phantom protest dissipates as the demoness approaches, pushed away by the power she commands. She never speaks, never replies to Shaw's heckling, but knowing she can do more for the coffin birth than us, we relinquish him to her care.

She takes the sinewy rope in her razorblade teeth, yanks until the navel string tears, and tosses the rotting placenta back into the grave. Her body emanates an otherworldly heat and her many breasts look full and ready to nourish, unlike the barren, cold, and collapsing body of the infant's mother still lying in the ground. The wicked wet nurse raises the boy to a tit and even though it's foreign milk, he suckles without discrimination.

"Which nipple do you think I chewed on as a newborn?" Shaw asks as she disappears into the blackness with the child. "I'm guessing middle right."

"With eight of them, you've got a twelve point five percent chance of being correct."

The graveyard is quiet again, save for a distant owl and the sharp, beginning squirts of the sprinkler system.

"That's the job then." Shaw makes a show of brushing the dirt and the responsibility of the child off of his hands as he begins walking away from the hole we've made in the ground.

"Whoa. You know it's not over until we put the dirt back. We don't get paid the eighty years of life we just earned unless we rebury the mother."

"You're no fun, Butcher."

"I'm plenty of fun, but this isn't it."

Shaw sighs and we refill the grave and replace the sod, leaving the plot about the same as we found it, minus the baby. As we walk back to the truck, we listen for the cries of the next child left destitute by death and displaced by decay. A large, black obelisk shines in the moonlight, demanding I stop to read it as I pass.

Shaw

"It's here! I found your grave!"

Shaw, nearly back to where we parked, doesn't turn to look. "Might be, but I still don't feel a thing!"

*"THE TROUBLE ABOUT JUMPING WAS THAT IF YOU DIDN'T
PICK THE RIGHT NUMBER OF STOREYS, YOU MIGHT
STILL BE ALIVE WHEN YOU HIT BOTTOM."
- SYLVIA PLATH, THE BELL JAR*

CLOVE HITCH

The morning of the day of my death, I try to give her my all. I caress her soft, warm skin in the darkness of our bedroom. We shower together and I shampoo her hair. She leans against the tile and closes her eyes, thoughtful or perhaps exhausted by the weight of my sudden tenderness, something that admittedly our marriage has been lacking. It too tires me. My hands cramp and the blood drains from my arms. Loving someone everyday takes so much effort, almost as much as deciding to leave them does. I'm eager for all this work to be history, to be summarized by a name on a memorial plaque. For once, I'm longing to be nothing more than a faceless, bodiless statistic of my choosing. Death over inevitable divorce, but under the guise of helping to save the overpopulated world.

Jena doesn't know I'd sided with the cause and signed up to end my life, that this breakfast is our last meal together, or that she'll be sleeping alone tonight. She doesn't know like she hadn't known about the credit card debt I'd amassed back in Phoenix before the endless droughts forced us north. Like she didn't know about the vasectomy I'd opted for even though, despite how hopeless everything was the world over, she selfishly still wanted children. I'd kept my impending noble suicide from her like I'd kept so many of the other important things. They were never little white lies. I was never a petty thief. They were always big, black, wicked ones, always the grand larcenies of withheld information.

It was difficult to tell her the hard stuff. Her temper was one bent on property damage, the type that dishes didn't survive, that sort of incoherent, physical rage that must destroy as much as possible before the crying begins in earnest. My wife, the tornado.

I didn't have the energy to calm her down, or dodge plateware, or to admit to everything after the unavoidable 'what *else* don't I know?' So I keep it from her. It's easier this way. Perhaps I signed up to be a martyr in a bid to cleanse my soul of all this sin.

During our last meal, gusts of wind carry the worship hymns of a congregation in a nearby church to our ears, a neat bonus feature when we bought the house. It's a faith that isn't ours, but calming nonetheless. She scratches at a spot on her scalp, somewhere I hadn't managed to rinse well enough and this small motion reminds me of all my failures, how I could never really love her properly, nowhere near how she deserved.

Despite my shortcomings, and as though the cup isn't the last survivor of a set she'd smashed last month, Jena manages the purest smile above her glass of orange juice. Tiny triangle shards still hide throughout the house, tracked by our socks, cutting into everything, waiting to do more damage at some later date.

She chugs the rest of the juice and hand-washes the glass with a grace and delicateness that suggest the cup should only be shattered with intention, never accidentally, revered up to the point of its planned annihilation. She takes the time to dry it with a hand towel and returns it to the cupboard from which it was pulled. On her way upstairs, she stops to kiss my cheek. I am left alone to listen to the faithful and ponder my death. I should be dead by midday, by the time service lets out, and if mine is a soul worth saving, may their hallelujahs lift it to the heaven in which they believe.

Above the rising and falling song, another noise joins in; a moaning accompaniment sorely out of time and tune. I follow the acoustic addition upstairs in an attempt to find its source. It's louder than the house itself has ever been, not a growing pain, nor a slow settling. It turns out to be a death lurch, an entire bloodline ending.

Jena hangs by her neck from the exposed beam in the ceiling at the foot of our bed. Urine seeps from the ankles of her fitted jeans. Her eyes are open, the bags beneath them somehow darker than when she was alive just moments ago. I should have noticed that she hadn't done her makeup this morning, that her hair had been cut recently, or at least that she'd stopped wearing her wedding ring. When was the last time she told me she loved me?

Shock then drops me to the floor, delayed like a tidal wave following an earthquake. My eyes close as the sound of the gentle swinging slows. My wife, the human metronome. I pick myself up and grab a towel for the cooling piss on the floor. Love, or at least marital obligation, compels me to get her body down. My feet sink into the bed as I wrap an arm around her waist and saw my pocketknife rhythmically across the rope. None of it makes sense. I didn't know we owned rope. When had she learned to tie a knot like this? I'd thought the beam, like her occasional sorrow, was decorative, not load-bearing, a feature without any heft and therefore not to be taken seriously.

We fall together to the floor and I want to ask about her head where it hits the wood and tell her how I've sprained my wrist trying to arrest our descent. Maybe we could laugh over the silliness of it, and the asparagus reek of her urine, and the gathered dust beneath the bed only visible from our spot on the ground, but her head is turned away, her eyes fixed on a far corner of a room I cannot see.

Jena and I exist on different ticker counters, separate census lines. The divide is unfathomable. It had looked so small on the television screen, the space between those who had signed up to die and those who'd gone ahead and ended things. Something sticks in my throat and quivers there, undulates in a thick ball, like a murmuration of birds, dense yet fluid above a quiet and empty field. I hold her for a few minutes, pull her poorly rinsed hair away from the torn skin of her neck, and cry. The choir sings on the wind and my sobs support the bass notes of a melody about hope as I mourn the loss of a woman without any.

I can't stand looking at the wetness on her pants, so I peel them off and redress her and pull her onto the bed.

I search everywhere for a letter, tear the house apart to the wiring for an answer I'll never have. Suddenly I understand Jena's intense outbursts. All I want to do is rip the whole damn world apart, shatter anything capable of breaking. *What else don't I know?* I wanted to scream it. How much else had she kept from me? The ransacking reveals nothing, not even a half-made grocery list, or a novel with a bookmark in it, or any leftovers in the fridge. Everything is done. That goddamn glass is dry in the cupboard. There is no continuation, no loose ends, nothing to return to. The entire house is ripe to end with a full stop.

Then, in the bathroom, beneath the waste in the small garbage can, under the wads of toilet paper, used Q-tips, and tampons, a plastic stick quietly declares Not Pregnant in soft purple text. *No life!* it voicelessly brays. She hadn't mentioned the test. Though I guess her tying a rope around her neck and stepping off our matrimonial bed might have been her screaming out the words. Not pregnant. No life. No life.

A heavy knock on the front door interrupts our demolition project. I toss the test back in the trash where it belongs and head downstairs, sweaty and very much alive.

"I'm here for two pickups. I have a Jena and a Matthew." The man's coveralls, clipboard, and the van parked on the street behind him all imply he's a repairman using nicknames for busted appliances and not a grim reaper here to collect bodies, but I've seen people like him on the news, doing this job just as he is doing it. Jena and I will fit nicely between the wheel wells in the cargo area, on top of the neighbors who opted in to opt out of life. We'll be driven to a cremation facility, burned back into oblivion, and honored on a wall in a park somewhere.

"So she *had* registered?" I ask him as though he's been scouring the house from chimney to sub basement with me, as though we, together, had been on the hunt for clues. It was an answer of some kind for me. Her plan was to die. It wasn't the news on the test in the trash. Not definitively anyway.

"I'm here for two pickups," he repeats, unable to break the conversation into something more human.

"Uh, right," I mumble, a bit annoyed. In all honesty, I'd forgotten about the scheduled pickup. It was one of the points of registering. At first, registration seemed silly. I could off myself whenever and however and as long as others followed suit, we'd be doing some collective good. I'd be one less hot shower every day, one less carbon footprint. Then, on the website, buried beneath the happy facts about the impact we'd all make, was a somber bit about the refuse of a dead body. The World Health Organization didn't want corpses left undiscovered to rot and spread disease, to slowly out their hiding spots through the scent of decay. Imagine millions of us making just another giant mess. So, registration assured pick up of my corpse. I look at my watch, half past noon. I should be dead right now. I'm late. The man at the door is right on time. I place a hand to my still-beating heart. "I'm Matthew."

"And Jena? Is she still alive in there too?" He looks behind me as though death is a game we play and Jena's simply hiding behind the couch, ready to spring out and shout 'surprise!'

"She's really dead," I explain in case he seriously expects some charade. "She's upstairs in the bedroom, on the bed. She looks like she's sleeping, but she isn't."

Talking about her like this, I expect to cry more, but somewhere between my planned offing, Jena's successful one, and my hunt through our home for lost knowledge, I've run out of tears and become a husk with only stringy remnants of viable emotion clinging to my hardened insides. I am a man without a map, lost and unable to ask for directions.

"If you're having second thoughts, that's absolutely normal." His face is the picture perfect rendition of sympathetic, as though he learned it from a chart of human expression.

"Oh, no, I'm definitely still going to do it. Jena, she... it was a surprise. We hadn't talked. I didn't know she'd registered."

He checks his notes. "But you're married aren't you?"

"Things have been strained." Having no more answer than he does, it's all I can think to say. It's a fact to which our dwindling dishware collection can attest.

He raises his eyebrows, something androids can't do. "Did she know that *you* registered?"

"No, but that's not the point. I wasn't prepared to find my wife's body hanging from the rafters, okay? I was going to be gone and that's it."

"Well, how was she going to find yours?"

"I have pills. From the internet."

"So, asphyxiated on your own vomit possibly with shit in your pants? Hopefully sitting on a plastic bag on the couch? That smell would never come out.

More human with every comment.

"You're right. I hadn't thought that far ahead."

"You'd have left her with a body, alone before lunch. May I come in?"

It's then I realize he's still on the porch, a sideways rain getting into the throat-to-crotch zipper of his uniform, the cold in a relentless search for his bones. "Sure, yeah. Come in."

He eyes the holes in the drywall, the exposed pipes and ductwork, and the brand-new cracks in my psyche.

Beads of perspiration emerge from the tree line of my hair and dash into my eyes like a frightened herd escaping something much bigger than them.

"What happened here?"

"As I recently stated, I found my wife dangling from a ceiling beam. It was a little upsetting."

"Must have been difficult. I'm sorry for your loss." The reply is clinical, a recitation, a pharmacist mumbling directions for a course of antibiotics, something they've said so many times the words bleed out without any heart. I like it better than the judgment. He writes something down.

I eye his clipboard, maneuver not-so-inconspicuously to glean information from its top sheet like a B-lister trying to crash an A-List party. Only I'm not looking for my name; I'm looking for Jena's. He pulls the clipboard against the wet chest of his coveralls and I fear for the ink on the page, fear it might run away as easily as she did, with any answers either held then rendered irretrievable.

"It's confidential, Matthew."

"Does it tell you when she registered? That's all I need to know. Does it say why?"

"Why would anyone sign up? To try to save the planet we've ruined."

"Be realistic. There are those using this program as assisted suicide, a way out. Anyone can lie. I do it all the time." I shrug and sigh.

He looks me over and notices, I'm sure, my greying hair and the deepening creases in my brow and heart. His eyes return to the form.

"Early March. Near the beginning of the open registration," he divulges, taking pity on a grieving man.

"That's just after we saw the announcement on TV. How did she live with me this entire time and not mention it?"

"Can't say. Never met her. How did you keep it from her? Oh, I see *you* only registered last week."

Was that a dig? I get the urge to grab the clipboard, but resist. "How would you have gotten in if we were both gone?"

"Lock picking classes. Every scenario has been accounted for. I'd have found a way."

"And if I decide not to follow through with it?"

"I'll kill you." He stops breathing and stares me dead in the eyes.

I feel strangely defensive for a man who wants to die anyway. I step back. He laughs.

"You had me there for a second."

"Really? I practiced that in my bathroom mirror, that serial killer look."

"It's good. You did good. Nearly gave me a heart attack."

"Wouldn't that be nice? Then you could get on with your whole dying thing."

I notice a thick briefcase at his side. "What's in it?"

"It's my one stop body dropping shop."

"What does that mean?"

"Guns, knives, poison. Everything one could need to end a life. Options for failed attempts."

"Seriously?"

He nods and checks his watch. "What's the plan? Should I wait or come back?"

"You'd stay while I…"

"I'm all about saving precious fuel and the planet.

We're all doing our part."

"But *you* didn't register?" I grab the opportunity to throw him back a little shade.

"No. I've got kids. I couldn't leave them behind with their mother."

"Jena wanted kids."

The reminiscing serves as his cue to pull me back to the tasks at hand.

"Would it help if we took her body out to the van?"

"Yes, I think so." Maybe the ghosts of her dreams would leave the house with her.

We find her where I left her, in a thicker darkness, permeated with that cloud of asparagus urine musk born of last night's dinner. I open the blinds, allowing the grey daylight to flood the room. Illuminated, she has transformed from a woman sleeping into a corpse. I crack the window to take a deeper set of my final breaths. Her dirtied jeans lie in a pile on the floor.

"Clove hitch," the man says as he points at the knot of rope still wrapped around the beam.

"Yeah, it's a hitch all right."

The body collector smiles. "That was funny, but it's impolite to laugh around the newly deceased."

It's not a rule I've ever heard, yet I nod because it sounds correct. I resent that he and my wife share knowledge of a knot. Perhaps her secrets lie folded in that specific combination of tucks and turns. It's somehow more complicated than that. I want more time alone with her body. It's the one place I didn't check for answers. It's a good thing he's standing closer to her than I am. I get the urge to pull open her mouth and scan for the truth stuck at her gum line. I want to strip her naked to be sure she's how I remember. I close my eyes and picture the skin of her back in the shower, how nothing was out of place. No suspect moles or marks. Everything was as it should be and how it had always been. No new truth was lodged in her post-breakfast smile.

"Did you want them?"

"What?"

"Kids. You said she did. Did you?"

I move back to the window and gasp for air.

"Whatever the answer is, she can't hear you."

His words are of little comfort. "I wasn't hearing her either."

Somehow I know he's checking his watch again. The floorboards creak under his shifting weight.

"I don't want to rush you, but I have other appointments to keep."

"Okay. How do we do this?"

"Take her ankles. I'll get the other end and lead."

Lifting her together, she feels insignificant, a piece of trash to be thrown out like the jeans she pissed through, a piece of furniture to be taken to the dump. My wife, the beat up loveseat.

There is no ceremony to us crossing over the threshold, no fanfare. Just two pall bearers who'd rather not be in the rain, one of whom is so close to death himself, and one unexpectedly dead woman who couldn't care less about the water hitting her face. Her neck looks terrible in the daylight. I drop my gaze and realize I never put on shoes.

He opens the double doors of the back of his death chariot.

"Oh!" I cry out and I nearly drop the one end of my

wife growing heavier in my hands. I was not prepared to see the dead faces of several of my neighbors, one corpse being more than enough for my midday.

"It's heavy, man." I'm not sure if he means the sight of a pile of bodies or the one we're still holding, but it doesn't matter either way.

"At least the weight of a hanging human body, yeah. Heavy." Tiny hairs poke through the compressed skin of Jena's ankles and stab into my palms. I'm reminded she is human, or was once.

"It's okay. It'll all be over soon," he says as he lifts my wife's shoulders into the van. They are more words that sound rehearsed or perhaps he's just said them too many times now every syllable flows wrong, so familiar they aren't anymore.

We position Jena against the wall and I extend one of her arms across the eyes of the bodies next to her to take away their power.

"Kinda crazy you two chose the same day to die without knowing it. That's got to be some kind of special spousal connection."

"Right. Special. She didn't even tell me about the test," I retort. He doesn't ask me to elaborate. He doesn't remind me I'm no better.

Back inside, the rainwater dripping from my hair, I remember the one thing left unfinished besides my own suicide. I return to my abandoned breakfast plate. He checks his watch again and I imagine bodies piling up in the streets, threatening to breach WHO protocol. I push the cold eggs around and snap the hardened bacon in half before dropping it all into the trash.

"I have to clean this up. Jena didn't leave a mess."

"There are holes in the walls, man, and piss on the floor upstairs. Nobody cares."

"No one cares?" I stop mid-scrub and step backward to turn and face him. My left foot finds another piece of our dishware. It cuts into my skin and somehow this connects me more to Jena than sharing our death day does. I wince and it's all I can do to not drop the soapy plate onto the floor to shatter like everything else. Not knowing about the tiny ceramic landmines, he mistakes my grimace as evidence of something different.

"I'm sorry, that's not what I meant. The whole world cares. This is a huge thing you're doing. Historic. Monumental. The dishes will be taken care of for you though. That's all I meant. Everything here will be taken care of." He swings his arm to gesture at our brokedown palace. "You only need to worry about taking care of yourself."

He's holding his clipboard again and my heart sinks when I realize he's crossed her name off his list. Everything becomes unfinished and I am not ready to have my own striked out.

"There's a lot of glass in the carpeting. Tell them that. It should probably be ripped out and replaced." The impulse to get a Band-Aid for my foot overwhelms me, but why tend to the wounds of a man bent on dying?

"I'll let them know," he says, but notes nothing.

"When you prepare her body, when you wash it, rinse her hair well. I didn't get all of the shampoo out."

"That's not my job, but I will let them know." Again, just words.

"They aren't going to prepare her body are they? They'll pull her out and throw her into an oven to burn."

"It's not my job. I don't know. Why are you delaying this?" he asks. "There will never be enough time to mourn her properly. It will hurt for as long as you live. You may as well cut that suffering short."

"After I'm gone, can you drive us by the church down the road?"

"Sure, man. Whatever you'd like. But I can't do my job until you do yours."

The wound on my foot is far too shallow for me to bleed out. And he's right about the heartache. That could take decades to destroy me.

"Okay. I'll get the pills," I concede.

I grab a few beers from the fridge as well, a brand I'd selected solely on its name of *Death's Head*. I'd felt clever as I'd pulled it from the cooler at the grocery store. Now, with an audience, I feel stupid and the idea, painfully contrived. It's all so imperfect, these final moments before my death and with Jena's final exit near poetry in comparison.

"I can sit next to you or I can wait outside or watch something on TV."

"I brought one for you." I hand the beer to him already open, making the choice for him to stay. The beer tastes better than I expect. My blood stains the living room carpet. He pretends to drink. I remember he's on the job.

"Having performance anxiety?"

He sets down his full beer. I drain the rest of mine.

"A little. I've never let someone watch me kill myself before."

"Good news is, you only have to do it once!" He laughs, which I suppose is okay to do around the not-yet-deceased.

I relax and sink deeper into the cushions. The pills

rattle against the bottle, a tiny death maraca signaling the last verse of a song. The pop of the lid, a hit of a drum for the finale.

"Should I take all of them?"

"Fuck it man, go big!" He hands me his beer and suddenly the body collector is an old friend, cheering me on to chug while we watch the game.

"All right. I'm doing this."

"Just as you planned."

I swallow alternating mouthfuls of pills and beer and my tongue catches hints of the bitterness. I remember the last time Jena told me she loved me. Months ago, after the first time we had sex once I'd had the vasectomy. She touched the small scar of the incision. I'd lied and told her my doctor had to remove a lump. That I didn't want to worry her by telling her before the procedure. That we could definitely still make babies.

"I feel pregnant," she said after the act. My wife, the immaculate conceiver.

"You can't know that," I replied, knowing myself that she couldn't be.

"I love you. You'll be a great dad."

I laughed then, because I couldn't even make her happy enough to keep our dishware in one piece.

"I love you." I say it to her now, wherever she is. I say it to the room full of things that reek of us, to the glass-sprinkled carpet that isn't baby safe, the cold eggs and the negative pregnancy test in their respective trash bins. One final truth prefaced by so many lies. So much easier than punching holes in the walls.

The body collector nods in recognition of its intended meaning, an old hat at hearing the dying words of mankind.

"Amen," I hear, but I can't tell if it's him replying or the distant congregation ending their last prayer.

My eyelids close and I dream of my reunion with Jena and try not to picture it as only my body wedged between hers and the cold metal of the van parked outside. Somewhere down the road, the born sinners leave their pews and exit the sanctuary for coffee in the basement below.

NANCY GONE WILD

On the night of her twenty-first birthday, after cake and presents—a silver cross necklace and a cashmere cardigan—and after at least three years of waiting for the right moment, Nancy prepares to tell her parents she's heading to Florida for Spring Break. And she's practiced those very words over and over, in the mirror, in the shower, in her bedroom in the dark at night when she's tucked away from their judgment. *Florida for Spring Break. Florida for Spring Break.* Hoping that, when it finally reaches their ears, the repetition might lend strength and a natural tone to the utterance.

If Nancy's parents were usual, a dad who golfs and day trades, a mother who gossips with other housewives and drinks too much wine, or some similarly banal parental combination out of upper-middle-class White suburbia, Florida for Spring Break wouldn't be such a huge deal. In some way it might even be expected that she'd pop her proverbial cherry on a weeklong trip such as that. And if Nancy owned retired pompoms, had yearbooks full of well wishes to revisit, had even ever once gone to public school, her parents might have paid for the ticket, encouraged her to take a friend or two, and bragged about it in advance to their friends. But Nancy's father Allen farms and reads only the newspaper chucked weekly onto the gravel drive leading up to their farmhouse, and Nancy's mother Barbara sings in the church choir, sings to the chickens, and sings to Nancy every night before bed since she was a child. Nancy hasn't even been kissed. In fact, she's well overdue for that first peck and so many other systematically denied rites of passage. If Nancy's parents were usual she wouldn't have had to *plan* telling them anything. But they weren't and so Nancy dreamed day and night of a world outside of their grasp and far beyond God's plans for her—both bricks in the walls that hold her back—though part of her thinks this urge, this yearning for life beyond her small world, might be something predestined, something he'd built-in when she was made. Maybe she was meant for bigger things than the farm, meant not to follow in her parents' footsteps, but instead to run far in the other direction.

So she'd saved up, pinched together her meager allowance, which was not much more than the feed she spread for the chickens every morning. She'd hidden the fact that she'd used a computer at the library to buy the ticket, hidden her excitement, and now it was only a matter of finding the right moment to break the news.

A few shots of whiskey warm her father. Her mother clears the table of the spent wrapping paper and ribbons, the empty boxes, and the plates covered in cake crumbs and melted ice cream, proof of some level of happiness in their home. Nancy's heart pounds in double time as the paper burns a hole in her back pocket, sending heat into her face. Her father notices the change.

"Are you all right, Nancy? Do you need some water?"

Her mother returns to the dining room and sees Nancy's flushed skin, mistakes the blooming redness for just another of Nancy's allergic reactions, and swiftly flips into a maternally-reserved level of panic mode. It's only when she starts looking for the EpiPen that Nancy says anything, remembers to breathe through the nerves, and the ruddiness lessens to something imperceptible beneath the amber glow of the light above the table.

"I'm fine. Thank you for the gifts. They're beautiful." She caresses the cashmere sweater on her lap, looking for her next words somewhere in the weave and even though she secretly feels called to abandon him, she thinks of her God and his words that have so often guided her.

Lying lips are an abomination to the Lord, but those who act faithfully are his delight.

Nancy knows he's right, but truth with a slight modification won't hurt her parents too much, not if she frames it correctly.

"I bought myself a retreat, as a present."

Her parents' brows raise. Nancy does nice things for others. She volunteers at the homeless shelter in town, she slaves in the farmhouse kitchen for the church bake sale. Nancy is a good girl, not a selfish one. A flash of guilt overtakes her and she momentarily doubts the decision she's spent years weighing.

Have I not commanded you? Be strong and courageous. Do not be afraid; do not be discouraged, for the Lord your God will be with you wherever you go.

Even in Florida, she thinks as she releases a long breath and steels herself for the next reveal.

She slips a folded piece of paper from her back pocket and sets it on the table in front of them. Her mother pecks at it with trepidatious fingers, as though the edges of the creased sheet might cut down to the bone if handled without care.

"What's this?"

Without his wife's fear, her father grabs the paper like he grabs the legs of birthing calves, firmly, head on, and with resolve for an end to the task. "An itinerary? Are these flights?"

"To Florida, for the retreat. The plane leaves tomorrow."

The words don't come out as Nancy planned, not as she rehearsed over and over, no mention of Spring Break, but at least she said Florida, a shade of the truth. She flashes a smile, hoping it serves to remind them it's good news she'll return from and not some permanent jump of their fledgling from the nest. Her mind flicks to the ways in which they might try to clip her wings and steal this promise of freedom now that she's divulged her plan.

"I don't know, Nance. Why would you want to go and do that?"

Snip.

Her father shakes his head in disapproval, fixing his gaze somewhere beyond the paper, on a small stain on the otherwise perfect lace of the tablecloth, a stain he hadn't noticed before.

"I thought you were saving that money for a car?"

Snip.

"What good is a car, Mom? There's nothing for miles

around! A plane will take me farther, to something!"

"Maybe that's not a good thing. Why Florida? Why so far away? What if something happens?"

Snip.

"I've never gone anywhere. I thought you'd be excited for me."

Her father tosses the itinerary into the middle of the table where, now leprous and unclean, no one dares touch the thing.

"It's not that we aren't excited. We want you to be happy, we do, dear. We just thought when you finally decided to leave, you'd be happy somewhere closer to home."

"Closer? There's nothing for miles! What's closer? The barn?"

It's at this point they speak only to one another. Nancy fades into the background and in her place sits the news she's given them, the bits of information they cling to in order to pick apart, to scrutinize and to hold up in comparison to their beliefs. Nancy spent a lifetime in compliance, never raising her voice, never questioning her parents' convictions, never challenging their authority. Her father's eyes remain fixed on the stain marring the lace, an imperfect mark there for years waiting to be noticed, finally screaming out for attention. Her mother grips the silver cross around her neck, caressing the chain it hangs from as one might a rosary, bewildered that her daughter could ever feel trapped.

At some point, maybe when Nancy snatches the paper off the table, or when the grandfather clock dongs a bellow somehow deeper than it was ever constructed to manage, the spell of confusion breaks and her parents return their focus to her. Nancy thinks only of lessening the shock of her unintentional blow and of stealing the scissors back before they render her flightless.

"It's a Christian retreat. I'll pray every day."

Again, a sliver of the truth. A former pastor runs the hostel. Prayer services are offered both morning and night as well as group dinners and a bible study on Thursday evenings. All of those services are of optional attendance, but it's fine print Nancy feels unobligated to mention.

"It's what's outside this retreat that we're worried about," her father counters.

"The sin, the temptation. The Devil lives in the city." Her mother still clutches her necklace, threatening the integrity of the delicate gold links making up the chain. "You're safe here on the farm."

It's a diatribe Nancy's God-fearing, neighbor-fearing, everything-fearing parents have given many times, a lecture on the physical moral binaries of farm and afar, good and bad respectively, as though the tree line holds back not only the wind, but the city-bred heathens, promiscuous, secular, and barbaric in their ways.

Nancy's mother beams, having found a compromise. "We could come with you! Wouldn't that be fun? A little family vacation."

"No!" Nancy's reply is too eager, so she explains it away. "I just want to experience something different. If you come it won't be different at all. It'll be more of this."

Her mother's smile fades. "What's wrong with this?"

Nancy can't find the words to explain the weight of the Trinity, the burden of Christianity, the late nights and early mornings of farm life to the two people who stuck her with all of it.

"Answer your mother, Nancy!" Her father smacks a farm-hardened hand onto the table and stands to his full height, the chair and his composure falling away behind him, but Nancy–cashmere clutched in her fists–is already halfway up the stairs to her room. She peeks into the walk-in closet hiding her packed suitcase and caresses the name tag hanging off the handle to confirm its existence.

Sometime later, after Nancy is in bed with the lights off, her mother comes to her bedside.

"You shouldn't rile up your father like that. You know his heart can't take it."

"The harder you make it to leave, Mom, the more this place feels like a prison."

Her mother sighs. "Look, we aren't going to stop you, Nance. You have the right to live your life how you want. But you have to promise to call us every day. Let us know when the plane lands. Leave the address of where you're staying. Bring your bible, wear sunscreen and a cover up."

"Even your well-wishes come with fine print."

"We can't help but worry about you. Just promise me that you'll be a good girl. We raised you better than to give into temptation."

"I promise."

"That's all I needed to hear. I wish you'd have given us more time to prepare, but your father and I will take you to the airport in the morning." Her mother squeezes her hand and kisses her forehead, but skips the usual lullaby.

Sleep is hard to come by as Nancy's mind thinks of all for which she hungers, the things she's been denied, knowledge that should have been hers already and Nancy wants to try it all, every single thing her parents and their religion forbid her from experiencing. Sex outside the covenant of marriage, drugs, and heavier music than Christian Rock. She has every intention of seeking temptation and giving into it, Jesus as copilot, Jesus as witness. Nancy wants to give him a reason for being nailed to that cross.

At the airport, her father grudgingly lugs Nancy's suitcase onto the scale. "What's in here, Nance? One of the cows?"

People stare at them and for the first time she sees her parents as others do: unkempt, rough around the edges, of the earth, as though no matter where they go, the farm comes with them. Dirt forever beneath their nails, the reek of manure and hay sunk deep into their skin.

"It's too heavy," the desk attendant grunts, offering no further instruction other than a sweeping motion with her hand indicating they should move it back off the scale. Once more her father grips the handle and relocates the heft of her daughter's eagerness to leave. They step to the side to let more experienced travelers up to the counter, the ones who weighed their luggage at home, precariously perched on bathroom scales, doing reverse math to perfect the poundage. Nancy unzips her suitcase, exposing her naivety to the terminal's already nosy crowd.

"Well here's your problem!" Her father points to the oversized logs of rolled up sweaters filling half the suitcase, and Nancy's favorite pair of heavier boots separating the knits from more Florida-appropriate pieces. She'd been trying to imagine a climate where warmer items weren't needed, but no matter how many traveler tips and weather forecasts she'd read, her North-Midwestern mind couldn't grasp the concept.

With her suitcase repacked and under the maximum weight requirement, Nancy says goodbye to her parents. Her mother, weighed down by worry and an armful of her daughter's winter clothes, kisses Nancy's forehead. "I know you want to reinvent yourself, but don't change too much, honey. God made you in his image, which is perfect."

"Your mother's right. God doesn't make mistakes!" Her father calls as she walks through security.

She boards the plane and can't help but think it's a bit like walking the ramp to the Ark, selected to carry on living while leaving her parents to fend for themselves against some coming flood.

As the plane takes off, Nancy feels a moment of fear. She clasps her hands in supplication as the earth falls farther away.

Keep me safe, my God, for in you I take refuge.

She watches His world pass by below as it morphs into one she's never seen before. The houses grow closer together. The cities sprawl like vines, intersecting and tangling into one another, their old borders blurred or disappeared altogether beneath the burgeoning populace. Eventually, palm trees replace the elms, the pines, and the hickories of her youth and as the plane lands she can't help but smile at the bursting fronds reaching upward toward the sun.

A shuttle brings her to the appropriately-named *Ray of Light* hostel, coated in a screaming yellow with multi-colored inspirational quotes hand-painted and exploding in all directions around the frame of the front doors.

A tan, brunette male, draped relaxedly over two thirds of a loveseat, looks up from a fashion magazine. "Hello, hot off the farm."

Nancy's cheeks burn red. "Is it that obvious?"

"Like you were plucked from that very dirt and dropped here."

"I guess you can take a girl off the farm, but not the farm off a girl."

"Oh honey, I'll try my damndest. I'm Barrett." As soon as he's greeted her he's upright and extending a hand. "Barrett's actually my last name. First name's John, but nobody calls me that."

She shakes his hand, noticing his polished nails. "Hi. Nancy. Everyone calls me that or Nance."

"Sooooo, what are you here to do, Nancy?"

"Anything. Everything."

He eyes her outfit, ill-fitted jeans and a frumpy blouse with a high neckline. "But not in that, right?"

"Well, no. It's too hot outside for this. I was thinking of getting something for the beach once I got here."

"Pick a bed. Drop your stuff. I know a few good places to shop. We can check you in later."

Barrett takes her to the boardwalk where they weave in and out of people and shops. She's never seen water so blue outside of photos, never seen so many beautiful people, so many miles of sand. Men with bulging muscles workout on the beach, stunning Nancy with their mass. Barrett too can't seem to look away, which surprises her.

"Wow." Barrett's gaze follows a shirtless man on rollerblades as he skates by.

"Wait. Are you g-?" Nancy can't bring herself to say the word. "But you're a Christian?"

"Darn straight. You'd have to beat the church out of

me."

"Why are you at the hostel?"

"Turns out the good Christian thing to do is to kick your son out of the house for liking dick."

"And I thought my relationship with my parents was complicated. I'm sorry."

"Oh, don't be. They didn't like me much even before they found out I was gay. It's better I got away from them. Come on. This place looks cute."

Inside the boutique, Barrett pulls a selection of clothing from the racks and pushes Nancy toward the curtain at the back.

"Try this on too." He tosses a black two-piece bathing suit over the top of the curtain.

Just the thought of the black bikini, short shorts, and skimpy tank top makes Nancy blush once more, but her curiosity consumes her and if she's going to play a sinner, she may as well look the part. She drops the farm to the floor, averting her eyes from her own nudity, gets momentarily tangled in the collection of straps and fashionable distressing, and looks up at a reflection she hardly recognizes.

"Are you going to show me?" Barrett asks from the small waiting area near the dressing room.

"I don't know. It's a lot of skin."

"Perfect! You'll blend right in!" He throws open the curtain before she can protest. She steps out and Barrett covers his mouth, a squeal of excitement escaping through his fingers.

"Okay, you're wearing that out of here. Don't even think about changing into anything else!"

The cashier scans the tags still hanging from the pieces

and Nancy watches the number grow on the register.

"I've never paid so much for so little fabric," she mutters. Barrett hears her and is quick to justify the purchases.

"It's an investment in fun. You can't put a price on happiness."

Nancy walks out and toward the beach in her new outfit with her new friend and with her old clothes stuffed beside her bible in her tote.

"So what are you really doing here?" Barrett asks from his seat beside her in the sand.

"I felt stuck at home. Restless. I prayed for something more."

"Careful what you ask for, Nancy. He's always listening."

"You sound like my parents."

"They can't be *all* bad. They're Christians after all." Barrett laughs at his own sarcasm. "Besides, they made you and I just can't get over how good you look!"

"My parents say I'm made in God's image, not theirs. To that I say He could have given me a larger chest and longer legs."

"Well God didn't have boobs, so they've got you there! But really, look how gorgeous you are! I don't think God was unkind. You are altogether beautiful, my darling; there is no flaw in you."

"Did you just quote the bible?"

"Song of Songs, Chapter 4, Verse 7. It's my mantra. Any time I feel down I find a mirror and repeat it until I believe it again. But if you want me to leave God out of it, well," he points at a woman down the beach. "Her tits are smaller than yours and her nose is horrendous, but she's owning it. It's called working with what you've got and you've got a lot, Nancy."

Nancy's phone vibrates against her leg. "My mom. She's calling."

"Don't answer it, just send her a text with a picture of the ocean."

The waves fill the camera's lens and Nancy manages a photo before more semi-nude strangers wander into frame.

They spend the entire day at the beach, eyeing more than a few of God's most beautiful creatures, many of them taking the pair in with equal interest.

The sun lowers, painting the sky and clouds incredible jewel tones, reminding Nancy of the stained-glass windows of her church. Bonfires glow in the distance and the smell of burning wood mixes with the saltwater scent of the air. At the water's edge, the ocean nibbles at her feet, a hundred thousand tiny baptisms. *It's nice*, Nancy thinks. *It's different, but not different enough.*

Barrett returns to her side after saying hello to some friends. "This has been fun, but I've got to get back to the hostel."

"For what?"

"Bible study starts in thirty minutes."

"Bible study?"

"It keeps me straight."

Nancy stares at him.

"It's a joke, Nancy. Straight...? Because I'm gay..? Ugh, anyway, my parents pay for me to stay here as long as I attend bible study and pray the gay away. So it's basically an all expense paid trip to the beach."

They share a taxi back to the hostel where Barrett offers his arm to Nancy, but she stays in the car.

"Oh no, bible study isn't for me right now. But hey, where can I go for a drink?"

"I was hoping you'd ask!" He leans in the window and says to the driver "take her to Sacrilege."

"Seriously?"

"Yes, Nancy. You won't regret it, especially if you're looking to see how the other half lives. All your godless heathens in one place."

"Sounds dangerous.'

"Only if having a good time is a crime. Byeeeee." Barrett waves her off as the taxi pulls away.

Deposited in front of the club, Nancy stares up at the backlit sign as it grows brighter against the evening. The Satanic font feels like it could violate her. She imagines the devilish barbs spiking the tips of the letters piercing her retina, and the curves, sexual and serpentine, snaking their way between her bathing suit and skin.

A text from her mother arrives, breaking her trance.

Goodnight! Rest well my angel!

You too. Goodnight. Nancy replies, though her night is only beginning.

"You coming in?" A gruff voice barks from the door.

Nancy nods and begins to move through the entryway. The man stops her.

"ID?"

"Huh?"

"You can't come in unless you're twenty-one. I need your ID."

"Right!" She pulls it from her bag and presents it like the recently awarded merit badge it is.

The bouncer examines the card. "You're a long way from home, Dorothy."

"I'll keep my eyes out for witches then," she retorts with a smile, but for a man referencing a story, he looks confused about the details.

Inside the doors, a long, dark hallway leads her to a large, red neon cross mounted upside down on a black wall. On either side of it, two arrow-shaped signs point in opposing directions. One reads 'Dance', the other 'Drink'. She chooses to dance and turns left, but when she emerges into the room it opens up and the bar is accessible anyway to her right where the dance floor ends.

An oversized painting of The Blessed Virgin Mary dominates the wall above the DJ booth, but Nancy's never seen her so portrayed. Mary's robes are pulled high above her waist and her legs are spread, displaying her unspoiled vagina to the room. Someone's rigged Christmas lights behind it to emit a holy glow around her sacred vulva, arguably the birthplace of an entire religion. Nancy averts her eyes, troubled by the mother of God's vulnerable position. No matter where she looks however, her mostly beloved Church is mocked and Satan is glorified. Between the feet of the people dancing she sees the thick, white lines of a giant pentagram. The unholy numbers 666 are printed on the top of the tables lining the walls. Nancy squeezes the plastic of her ID until it's sharp edges press into her palm, aware of how easy it will be to lose herself here.

Nancy feels faint and the weight of her bible pulls the strap of her bag into the tender skin of her scorched shoulder. She regrets not giving the tote to Barrett. From beneath her old clothes, she digs out her debit card and cellphone and tucks the bag in a dark corner of the bar where she suspects even she might have trouble finding it. Nancy clutches the cross hanging from her neck, takes a deep breath and disappears into the middle of the crowd on the dance floor. The pulsing music vibrates her bones. Bodies push against her. She stands still for a moment, allowing the assault as she allows herself to let go of God just a little bit.

When she tires of dancing she crosses the room to the bar. Nancy asks for water even though she wants a drink, not knowing where to begin in the miniature city of towering bottles in front of the mirror behind the counter. She sees her reflection there, at the center of the crowd, everyone boisterous around her calm purpose, a contemporary reenactment of The Last Supper, albeit a false Eucharist. As she sips, she reads the names of the alcohols and looks up mixed drinks on her phone. Above the cell screen, she can see the bartender standing in front of her, looking to turn her water into wine.

"You're the lady of the night," he says when she looks up.

"What do you mean?"

He leans in. "There's always at least one, a woman who catches the majority of the attention, and tonight that is you. Three of the gentlemen at the bar would like to buy you a drink."

"But I just got here."

He shrugs.

She looks down the line at the men illuminated by the neon cording running the length of the bar top. She recognizes the look on their faces, anticipation with a hint of expectation; a similar look as on her parents' faces as she was leaving, though toward entirely different ends.

"Three men offering gifts, huh?" Nancy laughs to herself, not expecting the bartender to understand the reference.

"So which one will you have?"

Nancy never had her choice of men, or drinks, or much of anything. The shots have always been called by her mother and father, by God and his book, not selected off a menu for quick consumption, and never called by ridiculous names.

"Do I have to choose one?"

The bartender laughs. "You can have them all if you like. I won't judge."

"Can you make this?" Nancy shows him the recipe on her cellphone. He examines the list of ingredients and considers his stock.

"The Weeping Jesus, huh?"

"If he isn't already crying, he will be after tonight."

"I never question my guests. If you want to explain further, go ahead. I'm a good listener. But for now," he smacks a palm onto the counter. "That drink is coming right up."

As the bartender digs a scoop of ice out of the bin, the first of the three men takes the empty stool to her left and swivels to face her. "Where are you from?" he asks as he looks her up and down in a way that suggests the swell of her breasts and the curves of her legs might provide that information.

"You don't think I'm from here?"

"I can tell by your sunburn you're not!"

Nancy looks down at her lobster-red thighs, aflame even in the dim light of the club. "It's bad, isn't it?"

"That skin is all coming off! You're going to peel into a new person."

The thought excites her. She aims to return home reborn, unrecognizable. A full body molt fits nicely into those plans. "Good. I'm ready!" she exclaims, being not the first of God's creatures,–the lizards, the spiders, the dogs–to endure a good shedding.

The man laughs and she smiles. He makes small talk and a point to flash his gold watch and rings, drawing attention to his fingers or wrist whenever he can. The Weeping Jesus goes down smoothly and before she can order another she feels a tap on her shoulder. She swivels her stool around to face the dance floor and a second man stands before her.

"Are you Nancy?" he asks.

"Yes. Who are you? And how do you know my name?"

"I'm Frank. Barrett told me you're looking for an experience."

Nancy wonders for a moment how much of her night Barrett plans to orchestrate from afar. She imagines him giddily texting friends on her behalf while half-listening to scripture at the hostel's bible study. Nancy nods at Frank who outstretches his arm, a small pill sits centered in his open palm.

"You'll like this." He points to the sky as he yells over the music. "It'll take you up!"

She looks at the ceiling. Nancy has spent her entire

life hoping to ascend to Heaven some day. Maybe there's more than one route. *Set your minds on things that are above, not on things that are on earth*, she thinks as she downs the pill, secretly hoping she'll sprout wings. The world changes and no difference exists between the sinners and the saints. She dances for hours, fueled by the drug and the alcohol.

Whether it's the liquor or the mystery pill lighting the fire, Nancy's libido rages, gripping her so tightly she almost can't breathe. All she can think of is finding air and a man.

Outside the club, the warm night surprises her. She checks her cell and sees missed calls from her mom. She's too drunk, too high to call back. She'll understand, she hopes, with a few details left omitted.

Motorcycles line the street. Small groups of large, leather-clad men stand around the machines, laughing and smoking, admiring each other's customizations. The men inside the club—lean-muscled, soft-skinned, and groomed to perfection—don't compare to these beasts. A man stands apart from the rest, discreetly sipping beer and watching the others. She'd seen him at the bar earlier, similarly separated from the crowd.

Nancy watches him lean his thick, hairy, tan body against the side of the club. He's nothing like the men in church, sat straight in the pews, their morals buttoned as high as their dress shirts. Curls of hair stick out from the top of his. The hair on his head nearly touches his shoulders. She's never seen a man as manly as him in real life. He looks like a farmhand pumped up on steroids and heavy metal music. She imagines his rough hands on her and can think of no holier blessing.

He sees her watching him. "Hey," he calls, "you

disappeared before I could buy you a drink." He tosses the empty beer bottle into a trash can and waves to her.

Nancy joins him near the end of the line of motorcycles. "I was dancing!"

He nods. "Half decent DJ tonight."

"Is one of these yours?" she asks.

He points to a pristine white motorcycle, the only white one of the group. Nancy perceives the color as pure, until she reads the hand-painted, flowing script on its gas tank. 'Conquest'.

She traces a finger down the machined curves of the bike. "Wow, it's beautiful!"

"Does more than look good. She's a hell of a ride. Care to join me?"

This is it, the moment Nancy has been waiting for, everything else has been a warm up. The flirting, the drinking, and the dancing could still be argued away, but this is her opportunity to choose between good and Godly and the evil her parents have tried so hard to keep her from. Never more has Nancy wished to distance herself from her shepherd and his flock.

"I'd like that. It's too early to go home, so where to?"

"Anywhere you'd like. Anywhere at all." The man sits down and takes a key from the pocket of his leather jacket.

"Let's ride around awhile and see where we end up!"

He nods and pats the padding of the seat behind him. Nancy swings a leg over the bike and rests her chest into his back, excited by her closeness to the stranger. The engine turns over and rumbles beneath her as the humid evening settles over them. She clings to him for what turns out to be a ride back to his condo.

"I've got a great view of downtown from here. It'd be

a shame for you not to see it."

"Did Barrett put you up to this?" Nancy giggles as they ride an elevator to one of the upper floors, only slightly afraid of the man's forwardness.

"Who's Barrett?" the man asks as he unlocks the door.

Nancy's too stunned by the condo to dwell on his reply. Where the farmhouse is mud-covered and utilitarian, and a mix of furniture and finishes, his pristine apartment collects no dust and even the handleless cabinets appear high-tech. Nothing looks easy to use, everything must require a trick. Nancy can't help but think there's more to this man as well, something he isn't letting on, but it grows her curiosity.

"Are you human? This place is immaculate."

The man chuckles. "I work a lot so I don't spend much time here. It keeps pretty clean by itself."

"Where do you work?"

"I own a bike shop. I build custom motorcycles for people with too much money. Merv's Machine Works."

"Merv?" Nancy asks incredulously. She'd expected him to be a Jesse or something similarly dripping with sex and machismo.

"Yup. Short for Mervin. So trust me, Merv is better. Would you like a drink?"

Nancy nods and takes a seat on the sprawling, white vinyl sofa. Her father would kill her if he knew she was alone in a man's home, her legs swinging over the seat of the couch in gleeful expectation like young Nancy, sitting in a pew, waiting for God's word to wash over her.

Merv brings her a full glass of red wine, which she's only ever had during communion. She sips it to find it's a much stronger concentration than whatever her church puts in the tiny cups, making the blood of Christ look like a shot of grape juice in comparison. The bitter blend pulls her cheeks in.

He sits next to her on the couch. "Do you like it? It's called Desecration."

"I'd like for you to desecrate me," Nancy mumbles and then gasps at her own mouth.

Merv clears his throat. "I'd love that, of course. But we also don't have to do anything. We can just hang out and enjoy the wine."

She considers the possibility of keeping her virginity in the face of an absolute opportunity to lose it. She takes another sip of wine and the boozy aphrodisiac solidifies her decision. "I was saving myself until marriage, but I've changed my mind."

"Just like that? Well lucky me," he says as he sets down his own glass of red. He pulls his shirt over his head, exposing his chest and a tattoo there. She touches a finger to trace the lines of the unfamiliar script.

"What is it?"

He points to the silver cross hanging on Nancy's upper chest. "Another kind of god. Maybe I can introduce you sometime. But for now, I have another old friend I'd like for you to meet."

Merv unzips his leather pants and frees his genitals and drunk, altered Nancy has no trouble finding the courage to touch it. She grips his hardness and tugs gently upwards. The motion reminds her of milking the cows, only in reverse. "Is this okay?" she asks, unsure of her technique.

"It's great, but I'd like more." He looks down at his stiff cock. "Clearly I'm ready if you are."

Each one must give as he has decided in his heart, not reluctantly or under compulsion, for God loves a cheerful giver.

"I'm ready." Nancy exhales before she gives herself away.

She's only been full of God's love before, only ever penetrated monthly by tampons and yearly by her gynecologist. Merv's cock feels better than Sunday service and he's deeper inside of her than Jesus has ever been.

Above all, love each other deeply, because love covers over a multitude of sins.

"Deeper!" she screams, hoping to push the rest of the Lord out; the holy trinity displaced by cock and balls.

The more Merv fucks her, the more he transforms from man to animal. She can't hear God anymore over his grunting and panting. He groans and she knows he's finished inside of her. Soon after he pulls out and looks at her with wild eyes.

"Can I go down on you?" he asks.

"Even though you jus-?"

He nods and smiles, his canines catching the light of the bedside lamp.

"Okay," Nancy answers.

His face disappears between her legs. He licks. He licks more. He bites. He bites harder. Nancy feels the heat building to a sharp crescendo, until it's no longer pleasurable.

"Ow!" she yelps.

Merv resurfaces. Cruor tinges his lips. He smiles, revealing blood-covered teeth. "It's just a little love bite. I'm sorry. I get excited."

Nancy looks down at her inner thigh and sees red there too. Maybe this was more experience than Nancy wanted. "I'm bleeding."

"It'll stop."

"It's going to leave a mark."

"A souvenir! Something to remember me by. We're bonded now."

Nancy finds it a funny thing to say after a one-night stand, but him being her first, she can't expect to know how things like this should go.

Merv dresses the wound, apologizing again as he does. "I'd ask you to stay, but I have to be up early."

"Oh yeah, totally." Nancy does her best to hide her disappointment at not being held in his arms.

Outside once more, she straddles the bike and spends the ride back adjusting to keep the pain in her thigh to a minimum. Merv drops her off outside the hostel.

"I'll keep in touch," he calls as he pulls away.

He's gone before she can ask how he'll do that when they didn't exchange numbers.

Nancy is grateful her walk of shame is a short one, from curb to door. The hostel is dark and she does her best to find her bed as quietly as possible, but the drinks, drugs, and damage to her body make it difficult to see or walk straight. She hits the mattress, exhausted, but already eager for tomorrow when she can tell Barrett about her night.

Nancy wakes around noon and peels the sweat-soaked, makeup-stained pillowcase from her face. She stares at the abomination painted there on the cotton. It's a mockery of a holy relic, in beige coverup, cherry red lipstick, and smoky black mascara, a collaboration between Grey Goose and Covergirl for a modern take on the Shroud of Turin. When she's able to sit up, her body screams over the resurrection as she examines the bite on her leg. Beneath the gauze, dried blood obscures the true damage. Someone comes into the room, but she's too engrossed with the hole in her thigh to pay them any attention.

"She has risen!" Barrett declares, breaking her concentration. Nancy pulls the bed sheet up to cover her wound and resists responding to his call.

"She has risen indeed, hallelujah…," he offers as he sits on the side of her bed. "Fuck, Nancy, you could at least pretend to be Christian."

"I *am* Christian. I don't need to pretend. I'm just sunburned and stayed out a bit late."

"Yeah, three days ago! You've been in and out of consciousness since then."

"Three days?" Nancy searches the bedding for her phone. "My parents are going to kill me."

Barrett points to a small table where Nancy's phone lies tethered to an outlet. "It died from all the texts and calls, but don't worry, I talked to your mom when she called the hostel, stopped her from flying out."

Scared for a moment, Nancy grips Barrett's arm and stares into his eyes. "Tell me everything you told her."

"I said we went out for Mexican on the first night you got here and you ended up with food poisoning, but that everyone here was taking care of you. I told her that it's pretty common for out-of-towners to have trouble stomaching the food of some of the local joints. The pastor bought my story too and repeated it to her like it was true."

"What else happened?"

"We did a prayer circle for you. You were saying crazy stuff. You barfed on the pastor. Mostly you slept and made weird noises, like a puppy, barking and whimpering in its dreams."

"I don't remember dreaming. I don't remember anything. It was more like I was dead."

"Well the proof is in the pudding, puddin'! You're very much alive and now that you know I kept your parents from changing that, are you going to tell me what happened to your leg?"

"No. It's private."

"Private? Come on! I could have easily been your Judas, but instead I saved your ass."

"It's nothing."

Barrett huffs. "You should put some antibiotic ointment on that 'nothing' before it gets infected."

Nancy holds her pounding head and rests her elbows on her knees. "God, deliver me from this headache."

Barrett scoffs.

"I didn't mean you. My head is killing me."

There's movement beyond her pained vision, followed by the sound of a faucet handle, running water, and ripping packaging. The headache amplifies every noise.

"Drink this," Barrett whispers as he holds a glass of water near her face. "It works a bit faster than prayer."

She watches two white tablets fizz and dance at the bottom of the cup, hissing like serpents, judging her. *Sssssssss* for sinner. *Sssssss* for sex addict. Nancy hisses back before acquiescing and chugging the bitter solution in admitted defeat.

Once the headache passes and Nancy can stand upright, she showers. The water stings her sunburn and the soap sends shockwaves from her wound through her body. She cleans off the blood to see just how much flesh is gone. She'd never lost so much skin and meat. Not even when she was twelve and the horse kicked her in the arm or when her hand got shut in the door of the tractor five years later. So much was missing; Merv must have swallowed a chunk of her. A shiver climbs her back. Maybe her parents were right about evil.

She tears her cellphone from the wall and dials her mother. The phone barely gets in one ring before the line picks up.

"Mom?"

"Oh thank God, Nancy! I thought you'd had an allergic reaction and died! We've been reading terrible stories. Two college girls named Angela and Sara, rest in peace, lost their lives in Florida just this week. That could have been you!"

"Mom, I don't mean to be callous, but Florida is a big state and people die all the time. I'm okay, it was just a really bad meal."

"Yes, that sweet boy Barrett told me everything! It's so good to hear your voice."

"I can't talk long. I'm still not feeling too well, but I'll be home tomorrow."

"Are you okay to fly? Could you come any sooner?"

"No, Mom. I have some things to take care of."

"Give it to God, dear, anything that you feel like you can't handle. He'll take care of it for you."

Nancy wants to give it to God, she wants to give everything from the last three and a half days right back to him. When her mother ends the call, a text comes through from an unknown number. *Welcome back!* it reads.

She considers replying to the message, asking who it's from, letting them know she didn't go anywhere, but instead, Nancy looks around for her bible, to seek solace in the words of her God.

"Barrett, have you seen my bag?"

"Not since the day at the beach and I don't think you brought it home."

"Crap. I left it at that club."

Outside, Nancy grudgingly waves down a cab and directs the driver to take her to Sacrilege.

The club is shuttered, rundown looking when it's neon lights are off and the faded facade faces the honest glare of the afternoon sun. She knocks on the locked door, calls the carefully deciphered phone number peeling off one of the blacked out-windows. It rings once then skips to a recorded message about hours and drink tickets and to press '0' to speak to someone to settle unpaid bar tabs. The last option a chink in the shabby, but otherwise impenetrable armor of the establishment, a way in. Nancy presses '0'. One more ring and she's connected.

"What's the last name on the card?"

"Hi, sorry, I don't have anything unpaid. I just forgot my bag a few nights ago and wanted to know if it's still there."

"Look, we aren't technically open. You can come back when we are. Hours are on the door."

The hours aren't on the door. They probably peeled off years ago.

"I know. I'm sorry, but I'm flying out tomorrow and there's something irreplaceable in it."

"Fine. You said a few nights ago? I've got a bag. Name two items. Assuming they weren't stolen. Looks a bit rifled through."

"A brown leather bible and a blue zip-up hoodie. There's also sunblock and map of downtown an-"

"Okay. You could have stopped at the bible. No one brings a bible to a bar–especially this bar–and lucky for you it looks like no one steals a bible from one either."

"I'm surprised! It's leatherbound."

"Yeah, the lord sure works in mysterious ways doesn't he." A dry cackle bursts through the receiver into Nancy's ear. The door opens a crack and the woman pokes out her head. Just like the front of the club, the daylight does no favors for the aging barmaid. Her foundation cakes in her wrinkles, her grey shows through at the roots of her jet-black hair. She hands Nancy her beach tote.

"Oh, God bless you!" The words slip out, a habit, but now, even though Nancy wants to mean them, they've lost their meaning. A familiar phrase turned foreign by overuse.

"Uh huh," the lady mutters as she begins to shut the door.

"Hey! Do you know Merv?"

The woman shrugs. "He'll have to tell you that."

Before Nancy can pry for more, the door is closed.

Nothing seems to be missing, though at some point during its time underneath the table her bag gained a drink cup sticky with sugary residue and someone's scrunchie with blonde hairs still gripped in its folds. She flips through the bible and finds no defacement. It's as perfect and whole as when she abandoned it, something she wishes she could say for herself.

Back at the hostel, Nancy changes into a pair of ill-fitting jeans and a demure top. The clothes feel heavy on her shoulders when compared to the near-weightless, thin-strapped tank tops and too-short jean cut-offs now piled on the floor. She picks up the barely worn clothes and drops them into the hostel's lost and found box.

"No! Uh uh!" Barrett runs to her. "What are you doing throwing those away?"

"I can't bring them back with me. My parents won't allow me to wear clothes like that."

"No offense but, they let you wear clothes like this? A blouse that hides your great boobs and jeans doing nothing good for your ass?"

They stare down in mourning at the discarded items now interred with a broken Walkman and a greasy pair of sunglasses. Barrett clears his throat and begins to sing. "Amazinggggg Grac-"

Nancy smacks his arm. "Knock it off! They're just clothes."

"Farewell to 'Cool Nancy', briefly known and loved."

"Are you done?"

"I don't know. I might start crying. I haven't been to many funerals."

"I'm still alive. I'm standing right next to you."

"I'll miss you, Nancy. You remind me of me a few years back."

"How so?"

"Eager to leave the church behind, but one epiphany away from finding yourself closer to God than you've ever been before."

On the plane home, she watches the colors change from the lush, brilliant greens and blues of the Sunshine state to the drab browns of the Northern Midwest farmland. And though it's a daytime flight, as the wings cut through the clouds she feels particularly close to the moon. Nancy notices something else, even with headphones on she can hear the quiet conversations of those around her. She can smell the unique body odors of everyone on the plane.

How strange, Nancy thinks.

Nancy claims her shabby suitcase from the baggage carousel. She can hear her parents across the terminal and feel their giddiness over her return as an electric energy in the air that leads her to their place in the crowd. With her senses strangely heightened, Nancy still smells the sex on her skin and the remnants of alcohol on her breath. There's a moment of panic that her mother will smell it too, that her father will sense these new additions to her composition, and once discovered for having eaten the apple from the Garden, they'll cast her out beyond the gates, naked, abandoned, judged.

"Oh Nancy!" her mother waves so frantically that Nancy fears she'll need reconstructive surgery of her wrist. "I thought we'd lost you!"

They move in to caress her hair, hug her, interrogate her. The walls of her parents' love—more stifling than the Florida humidity—threaten her new autonomy. She pulls away, grimaces at their now alien touch as though their holy skin might set her tarnished flesh ablaze. Too, they've lost their familiarity. She knows who they are, but nothing inside her still feels anything for them, save for some small amount of pity that they don't know the world as she's beginning to know it. She left her love for them somewhere back in Florida. At the beach, in the club, on Merv's couch and cock, drowned deep at the bottom of that bottle of unblessed wine. She reaches inside herself for the happy falsetto voice they'll be expecting, musters the naive optimism they love so much.

"Hi! Hi!" She parks her luggage between them. "It's so good to see you!"

Her father embraces her before she can dodge out of the way again. He hasn't showered the morning chores off his body, nor has he changed his clothes. Hay and urine. Mud and chicken shit. That was his cologne. Nancy slides from his arms to gain distance from the acrid, pungent burn of his scent.

"Come on, give your Pa a hug!"

"Sorry, my sunburn is a bit raw and I'm really not feeling well yet."

"All right then, there'll be plenty of time for hugs once you mend. Let's get you home."

She sits crammed between them on the bench seat of the truck, enduring question after question about her trip.

"How was the hotel? And prayer service?"

"Did you make any friends?"

The interrogation continues until they're nearly back to the farm, until Nancy screams when she sees something sitting in the road in the distance.

"Dad, it's a rabbit! Stop!"

"What are you talking about? I don't see anything."

"Up by the top of the hill."

"Nancy, that's a quarter of a mile." His foot remains on the accelerator, with no action to ease its depression, until the hare is under the wheels, pulverized between rubber and gravel.

"Sure enough," her father says in the driveway as he picks

pieces of muscle and tufts of fur out of the tread with a stick. "How'd you see it so far away?"

But Nancy's standing at the front door, hesitant to turn the knob. Arriving back to the farmhouse feels like willingly walking into a trap. Nancy steps over the threshold, securing her ankle in the snare.

"Rest up! There's a lot of work that needs doing now that you're back." Her father reminds her before he returns to his paper and his coffee, both left idling on the dining room table while they picked her up from the airport. Her mother sits in one of the oversized reclining chairs in the living room and restarts her crochet project, sweaters for the chickens. Back to boring business as usual and the dull, slow progression of life on the farm.

She pulls her luggage up the narrow staircase to her room. There, safe, she breathes to slow her pounding heart. She lifts her bible from the depths of her bag, brushes the sand from it, and sets it back in its home on the nightstand. God had been her best friend and confidant since she could talk, but it's been almost a week since she's read his words. Now, like her parents, he feels like a stranger. She caresses the supple leather cover, aching for a reconnection to anything around her.

"Lord, help me," she pleads.

But Nancy's God is quiet.

Each passing day finds her more agitated and lost. She attributes it to the upward hormonal swing of her approaching period, but the blood never comes. A different thought crosses her mind.

Be fruitful and increase in number; fill the earth and subdue it.

But Nancy isn't ready to be fruitful. She sends a quick

prayer skyward, whether he's listening anymore or not, her hands clasped tighter than any previous ask. "God, please don't let me be pregnant."

Nancy does what she can to distract her mind until she can take a test, but everything reminds her of what she's missing about her Florida trip. *Not pregnant, not pregnant, not pregnant* becomes her new mantra as she milks the cows and thinks of Merv's cock in her hand. The handle of her hairbrush and, on occasion, a well-washed cucumber take his place inside of her. The drafts in the farmhouse make her body ache for the breezes blowing off the saltwater waves of the Atlantic. She sneaks sips of her father's whiskey to relive a small amount of the thrill of freedom she had on spring break as she stands close to the farm machinery to feel the bass notes of their roar in her bones.

"Stop fidgeting!" her mother snaps as Nancy shifts from butt cheek to butt cheek in the pew beside her. Nancy's uncomfortable from the ache in her thigh, uncomfortable with the words of the sermon, an entire lecture about the holiness of remaining chaste.

When the collection plate comes around, she takes it as usual to drop in a dollar, something she'd done since she was small, but on contact, the tithing bowl sears her hand as though the metal is hot. Nancy drops it and the money of the congregation scatters on the patterned carpet beneath her feet.

"I can't take you anywhere, Nancy!" her mother scolds, bending down to help her daughter recollect the spilt offerings. "And where's your necklace? The one we gave you for your birthday?"

Nancy raises a hand to where it should be hanging

from her neck. She'd taken it off and stuffed it in the back of her sock drawer when the silver started burning her skin, just as the silver of the tithing bowl had her hand, but that wasn't something she could admit to her mother, who might jump to calling an exorcist. "I must have lost it somehow."

"It was a gift, Nancy! How could you lose it?"

"I didn't mean to!"

"You used to care more. About everything. How will you keep God close?"

"God doesn't live in a piece of jewelry."

"How will you promote Christ's love wherever you go?"

"I'm not a billboard, Mom."

"Our lives are the mission. Everything we do is a reflection of him."

"I wish you, and HIM, would stay out of my business!" Nancy barks sideways at her mother's face before they both sit upright. Barbara passes the plate to Nancy's father.

"You're different, Nancy. A bit too reinvented," she whispers, keeping her eyes to the front of the church.

"I'm still me! Nothing is the same here though!"

"The farm is exactly as you left it. The church is too. The only thing that's changed is you. These are your clothes, but that's about it. The light's gone from your eyes. God's gone from your heart. You should have stayed home."

Her father, having passed the tithing bowl to his right, joins the conversation. "You could have stayed with the Andersons down the road. They've got that bed and breakfast."

"Not helpful, Allen."

"Look at me! I'm all worked up before the choir

performance."

"Time for church, Nance!" her mother calls up the stairwell on another morning in the farmhouse.

The light hurts Nancy's eyes and the smell of coffee- as strong as though it's been brewed beneath her nose- drifts into her nostrils, turning her stomach. She holds back vomit. The darkness of the walk-in closet calls to her growing nocturnal sensibilities. Nancy can barely look at the small rectangle of light cast by her phone, but she needs to figure out what's happening to her. She manages to type a text to Barrett.

What do you know about Club Sacrilege?

She waits for his reply, watches the letters of each word wiggle and rearrange themselves, listening to the bones in her mother's feet creak as she climbs the stairs.

"Honey, we're leaving." Her mother's voice is closer now, in her room, just outside the closet door. "It smells horrible in here, like a wet dog died. Nancy?"

The chime of Barrett's response betrays Nancy's hiding spot. Her mother pushes open the closet door.

"What are you doing in here?" Barbara covers her nose from the stench.

"Hiding from a migraine. Didn't we just go to church?"

"That was a week ago."

"We're either going to church or coming from church and frankly I'm sick of it. I can't sit in that sanctuary for one more speech about all the ways we as humans are terrible!"

"Fine. I won't take you anyway if this is the mood you're in. You should get back into bed and put down your phone. Maybe open a window. I'll pray for you."

Nancy nods, knowing little more than that she needs more than the pleas of her mother to save her. Still, she does as her mother says, but beneath the bedding she reads and replies to Barrett's message.

You said you wanted a life-changing experience. I made sure you had a chance at getting one. Then you came back to the hostel wounded and basically dead for three days so you're welcome.

A man bit me! And now all sorts of crazy stuff is happening!

Whoa! I didn't tell anyone to do that. What else is going on?

My entire body aches. I'm sleeping all day. I can hear and smell everything. I don't feel right. It's like I'm a vampire or something.

Well you don't need to worry, the only vampires here are the Scientologists!

Ha ha.

Have you tried calling the club? Or the guy who did the damage?

The club won't take my calls. I never got Merv's number.

I can ask around if you want

Could you? That would be great.

Nancy falls into a deep sleep, nestled in her blankets pulled tightly around her into a fabric den, until they're yanked free later that day. Her mother stands over her, still in her

Sunday best, scowling.

"You missed church and you've slept all day. You know this kind of behavior won't be tolerated, not by me and especially not by your father. This isn't Florida. This isn't Spring Break. There are chores to do, Nancy. Now change your clothes and go collect the eggs."

The door of the coop squeaks open and the scent of the earth, mixed with the smell of the birds and their shit awakens something inside of her. Nancy drops the basket, snarls, and lunges into the narrow passage between the rows of nest boxes, sending most of the chickens scattering for safety. As fast as she can grab them, Nancy crushes the roughly thirty, freshly laid eggs into her mouth, savoring the silky insides of the unfertilized brood as they slide down her throat.

Shortly after, Nancy comes through the back door, toting the empty basket with a hand smeared in broken yolks.

"That was fast. Were there no eggs?" her mother asks from her post at the sink, where she washes up their dinner dishes, her back turned to Nancy.

Nancy doesn't answer, causing her mother to face her.

"What have you done?"

A piece of shell detaches from a strand of albumen hanging from Nancy's mouth and lands on the linoleum. Other shards of multi-colored shell speckle her slime-coated arms. She stands still, unanswering, tarred and feathered in the carnage.

Barbara throws the sponge into the soapy water of the sink behind her. "Nancy, what happened?" she screams, hoping to break her daughter from her embryonic daze.

"I was hungry."

"That's disgusting! What has gotten into you?"

"You wouldn't understand."

"That may be true and I might not be able to see what you're hiding, but God knows. He sees everything! Go to your room!"

"I'm not a child anymore."

"You're right! You're something else entirely!"

"What's all the yelling about?" her father asks as he lugs two buckets of milk in from the barn.

"Nancy's having some kind of episode! She needs a shower and she needs to get out of my sight!"

"You heard your mother. Go on."

"You should be happy I spared the hens!" Nancy screeches down the stairwell.

Her parents stop asking her down for dinner and soon Nancy can't keep the food down anyway. Nancy starts pulling out her hair from a scalp that doesn't feel like her own. She can't keep herself from picking the sunburned skin off her body, even when the peeling causes bleeding.

Therefore we do not lose heart. Though outwardly we are wasting away, yet inwardly we are being renewed day by day.

No part of Nancy feels renewed. Her insides are crawling out and her outsides are falling off, making way for whatever works at surfacing. She tells herself it's part of God's plan and his just happens to be a particularly perverse divine providence.

Nancy's mother sweeps up hair and small swatches of her daughter's skin from the staircase, empties bowls of her daughter's vomit into the toilet, still reeking of the undigested meal, into the toilet. "I thought maybe this could be a new allergy, but you're falling apart, literally falling apart and straying further from God. Your bible hasn't moved from the bedside table since you came home from Florida."

"Didn't God make me in his image? Aren't I pretty, Mom?" Nancy grins, exposing her bleeding gums.

I'm taking you to talk to the Pastor."

"He can't help."

"Nancy, 'whoever conceals their sins does not prosper, but the one who confesses and renounces them finds mercy'. You're going and you'll tell him everything you can't tell me."

"It's sundown. He's probably eating dinner."

"The pastor, like God, is always available. All we have to do is ask."

Barbara dials a number she shouldn't know by heart. It rings a few times, then goes to voicemail. She hangs up and dials again.

"Father Powell, it's Barb."

"Barb, I'm eating."

"It's an emergency. Nancy's not right. I need you to meet her at the church. She has some things she needs to talk about." Barbara turns away from Nancy and whispers, "and when you see her, don't be afraid." She hangs up before Father Powell can ask for clarification. "Get in the truck, Nance!"

"I'll pick you up in an hour!" Barbara yells across the bench seat and out the passenger side window of the truck.

Nancy's at the church doors before the pastor. A text comes in from Barrett.

He's the leader of Lobos Loco, a motorcycle club that only rides at night. Merv's nickname is Death.

She rereads the last word, trying to make sense of how someone so sweet could end up with such a moniker. Another text comes in.

His bike is outside the club tonight, but the club is closed for a private event. They wouldn't let me in.

The pastor arrives. Small globs of mashed potatoes cling to his beard and chunks of steak fill the gaps in his teeth. He stares at her face, mostly illuminated by a small lamp above the arc of the doors, struck by how thick her skin looks, the breaks in it, the missing hair on her scalp, and how her lower eyelids sags, making her face appear like an ill-fitting costume mask.

Father Powell remembers Barbara's words, but can't help but feel a tiny trepidation. Sometimes people seek God when they should really seek a physician.

Nancy pockets her phone. "I'm sorry about my mom," she says to break the silence and his gaze.

"A mother's worry is a powerful force, much like the microwave that will reheat my dinner when I get back home. Come inside."

Father Powell unlocks the doors and leads her down the center aisle of the church.

"Your mother has asked me to do a few things while you're here, as much as I can really, to help you get right with God. Basically a spa day for the spirit. Sit and take off your shoes. I'll be right back."

It's not the first time Nancy's had her feet washed in the church, so the request isn't odd. She takes a seat on one of the front pews and removes her sneakers and socks, trying to ignore that several of her toenails have come off with the cotton. The pastor returns with a bowl of water and a few folded hand towels. He's grateful for a task that takes her face out of his vision, but then he sees that her feet are no better. She winces as the warm liquid envelops the exposed, raw skin of her toenail beds. Columns of blood curl and drift upward as layers of flesh separate from her foot like sheets of puff pastry.

"Oh!" He exclaims as he places the sheet of skin back on her foot and pats it with the towel as though it'll be enough to keep it in position. "There we go. All better. Let's move onto your baptism."

"I'm already baptized."

"For all the sin thereafter then. It won't hurt anything to do it again." He holds out his hand to help her down the stairs into the baptismal pool, worried about introducing more water to her unstable body. The lightly heated water soaks her wool dress and her aching joints welcome the partial weightlessness accompanying the submersion.

"He that believeth and is baptized shall be saved!" Father Powell proclaims into the depths of the empty church. "I baptize you in the name of the Father, the Son, and the Holy Spirit!"

He places a hand on Nancy's head and pushes her beneath the surface of the pool. She opens her eyes underwater and watches small snakes of her hair swim away from the dunking. The patch of skin from her foot detaches once more and floats away to rest on the drain grate at the center of the pool. She emerges partially bald with the remaining hair in dark strings clinging to her face and head. He makes a mental note to have the pool cleaned as he offers her a hand up the steps. The skin of her fingers begins to slip off in his grip, like a loose glove. He pulls his hand away and leaves her to manage the rest of the stairs alone.

Father Powell towels himself and picks coils of her hair off his clothing.

"Time for communion, I think." He gestures for her to kneel before the altar.

"It's not a good idea," Nancy says, "I haven't been able to keep anything down for a few days."

"We have to try." Father Powell is a physician offering trial drugs to a terminal patient, not ready to give up hope in his institution or faith in the medicines it creates. He presents the wafer, dry and colorless, and waits for Nancy to open her mouth to receive it. She shakes her head and refuses the offering.

"This is my body given for you; Do this in remembrance of me," he recites.

Again she denies him.

"You would refuse the body of Christ, Nancy?"

"I can feel it coming up my throat just looking at it."

"He died for you."

"He's going to kill me if you make me eat him!"

"TAKE AND EAT!" Father Powell wails, the command bouncing off the church's stained glass windows and painted ceilings. He pries her mouth open and feels the teeth inside giving way like dominoes in front of his fingers. Nancy vomits before the wafer touches her tongue. Teeth and the disc of unleavened bread fall to the floor.

"Fuck!" Nancy yells.

"Forgive me, child. I don't know what came over me. Let's get your confession done and have your mother come for you."

Father Powell considers having the conversation on a

pew, but can't bear the sight of Nancy if one of the rays of moonlight catches her deformed visage, made more horrifying by his acts of attempted salvation. He turns her toward the confessional booths and he can tell by her hesitation that she thinks it's a strange decision.

"I find people feel more free to talk when they can't see my face," he lies.

She raises a gnarled hand to pull open the swinging door of the booth. Father Powell shudders, but catches himself.

The Lord sees not as man sees: man looks on the outward appearance, but the Lord looks on the heart.

He wants to come out and ask Nancy what has really happened to her, but it seems like admitting she looks like a monster. It's good she stayed home from service. No one deserves to be a spectacle at nine in the morning on a Sunday.

"Nancy, it's been some time since we've seen you and now your mother has some concerns?"

"I haven't felt very well since I got home from Florida."

Both Nancy and Father Powell realize it's an understatement.

"Did something happen on your vacation?"

"I did things I shouldn't have. Probably broke a few commandments."

"Straying is natural and it's completely normal for a young woman like yourself to experience urges as the body matures."

"That's just it. I don't feel like I'm maturing. I'm turning into something else. Something not human."

He laughs. "Is there a possibility you're with child? Women experience pregnancy differently. Hair loss, skin disorders, changes in mood and sleep patterns, feelings of...otherness."

Nancy hears the steak digesting in his stomach, the mites crawling on his eyelashes. She hears the settling engine of his car parked outside. She hears nothing inside of her belly.

"No. The tests were all negative. It's more than that. I feel uncomfortable. Not uncomfortable in my clothes, but in my skin, like I'm layered up, like it needs to come off. I want to pull it off."

"Your skin?"

"It doesn't feel like my own anymore."

His heart rate changes, quickens. She's making him nervous. More so, she's making herself nervous. It's not normal to hear people's hearts. Nor is it normal to want to remove all of your flesh. Her teeth chatter, not from the cold, she's burning up as a vibration courses through her body.

"Have you taken drugs tonight, Nancy?"

"I wish." The words fall out of her splitting, scabrous lips. She raises a finger to touch the breaking flesh and pulls it away wet with blood. Drugs would make the vermilion tint of her fingertip rise and dance, they'd bring her closer to some god other than the one who has so clearly abandoned her, drugs would make music out of the clattering of her teeth falling from her gums and onto the floor.

"Are you all right in there?" He presses his nose up to the small screen set in the wall between them, attempting to make sense of the noise.

She's not all right. She's all wrong. Something inside of her claws to escape.

"I know what's inside of me."

"You're not making sense, Nancy."

"It's me, trying to get out."

Moonlight enters the sanctuary and the changes in Nancy's body begin in earnest. She lifts her dress and picks at the bite on her thigh, pulling hard on the edge of the wound until her skin releases and reveals a gleaming, soft fur beneath.

"I'm scared." Her voice comes out in a rough growl as her tongue and jaw elongate and her teeth extend to daggers. She drops her flesh on the floor of the booth, piling her old self on the blessed wood of the confessional.

"Trust in the Lord with all your heart and lean not on your own understanding; in all your ways submit to him, and he will make your paths straight," Father Powell recites. "There's nothing to be scared of," he whispers, the frantic rhythm of his heart once again betraying his words and exposing his true thoughts.

"Then why are you so afraid?" she asks with the last bits of her human mind as she relinquishes control to the beast within. She turns her blazing eyes outside to a new idol, the full moon. Her transformed body quivers in orgasm at the sight of the celestial spectacle and something new emerges from her throat. Another language. A different holy script.

A howl.

"Nancy?"

The pastor opens the door to the confessional booth, wherein sits a wolf in a wool dress, until it lunges forward to tear open his neck and break another commandment. Blood spurts from his jugular, wetting her coat in a crimson rush of dark baptism.

This is your body, given for me, she thinks as she consumes him. The meat stays down. The bones lie piled atop her old skin. She noses the church door open into the night, not pregnant at all, but reborn.

Full of his blood and flesh, her latent lycanthropy now fully manifested, she takes the shadows home on all fours, cell phone gently gripped between her pointy teeth. When the concrete ends and the gravel and dirt of the farm begin, she stops for a moment to pant and ponder this new perspective. She's never seen the farm from this level, never caught the scent of everyone who has ever travelled the road. The choking decay of the rabbit caught beneath the wheels of her father's truck haunts the air. A text message chimes, reminding her she has her phone in her jaw. She drops it where she can find it later, near a large tree at the head of the driveway.

Nancy runs through the fields and woods all night, between the old farmhouses, a creature of second coming skirting towering monuments to dying ways. She drinks from the pond and laps up the true meaning of her old god's words with every tongueful.

Wild beasts honor me, jackals and ostriches, for I put water in the desert and rivers in the wasteland for my chosen people to drink.

She feels chosen. She feels right under His domed sky. God made beasts and man and her. She feels something else as well, a kinship to the man a thousand miles away who made her into this creature. She howls and many voices howl back, an entire distant pack, yet somehow, even thousands of miles away, she hears and knows Merv's call perfectly within the chorus. She understands the meaning of the script tattooed on his chest. She knows the god he spoke of and she can't dispute the ancient, Arcadian king's existence as his power flows through her veins.

She stalks the perimeter of the farmhouse. The one she should have been home to hours ago, the one she should have left years ago. Through the windows she watches her parents make panicked prayers to God and frantic phone calls to men in search of her. If she hadn't consumed the pastor, she'd break through the glass and kill them both. Another time maybe, when her appetite returns with the next full moon.

Later, from the middle of one of the fields, she listens to her mother cry and sing to her empty bed. Nancy falls asleep to that familiar melody, curled in a ball, her tail covering her snout.

The moon disappears from the sky and as the sun rises, the wolf in her recedes. She shakes the lupine hair in sheets to the dirt, revealing new, pale skin. Her teeth and claws retract to a human shape and length. She stumbles across the last field to home, momentarily clumsy on her returned bipedal footing. Scraps of her wool dress barely cover her body, and spiky balls of burdock seed tangle in her long, brown hair.

She finds her phone and checks the text from the same unknown number. Beneath the *Welcome back!* message she reads:

Solve et coagula, my dear. How was THAT for a rebirth?! xxx Merv

Out with the old and in with the new, she replies. Thanks for the souvenir! ;)

On the morning after her first full moon, after her first taste of transformation and blood, she lets herself into the farmhouse, feeling youthful, vibrant, and strong.

The wolf shall dwell with the lamb, she thinks as she smiles, bits of the pastor and his steak still crammed between her teeth.

NOCHE OSCURA

I've turned the wheel toward the countryside, watched the houses grow farther apart, the trees take back the hillsides, and the fields start opening up to the sky. I'm driving to get away, destinationless, but determined to end up somewhere else before heading back to my reality. It's a therapeutic pleasure the rising gas prices stopped me from decades ago. Today, no matter the cost of fuel, my troubles demand I leave them behind to confront on one of my tomorrows. I'm choosing flight, having fought long enough. I haven't looked at the fuel gauge once, but it's the only amount of carefree I'll achieve. I religiously check my phone for any sign of life from my wife and our marriage I'm ending. There's nothing from her, only my father calling over and over, filling the voicemail box with heavy, long-winded rants about commitment, telling me more than I want to know about him and my mother's tumultuous, yet enduring relationship. He likes my wife for me more than I do.

The length of this empty stretch of highway is

unknown to me, as is, apparently, the long-windedness of my need for escape. I drive forever. Time passes as easily as the mile markers flick by, as seamlessly as the DJ's change shifts on the radio, each with that same smooth voice of a friend who knows exactly what to play. I nod my head in time with the beat of song after recognizable song until a cramp in my right leg threatens to seize my pedal foot and I notice the aching in both of my ass cheeks, physical suggestions that I've been on the road for hours, listening to the Top Forty replay without end. I wiggle my toes to remind my blood to flow. I clench everything and release. I twist and squirm in the confines of the driver's seat, but nothing eases the pain. The approaching U-Pick Pumpkin Patch—the only hint of life for most of my drive—seems as good a place as any to stop and stretch my legs or let them fall off and be done with it all. A rusty sign points down a long dirt road, which, the nearly empty parking lot reveals, only a few cars have braved. I notice right away the lack of the normal, bustling chaos of the patches closer to town. No policemen direct traffic here, no children dart without caution in front of me as I select a spot. No cider stands, no corn mazes, nor lawn games, only a pumpkin patch extending to the hillside on the most distant horizon in front of me.

Some things feel right enough for me to leave my car and approach the patch proper. The large barn to the right of the field is the bright, saturated red I expect, with just enough wear to support the idea that the farm is a working one. The cows all point south in some silent agreement with the magnetic field. Vines tie the pumpkins to the earth; not one of them has been loaded in on trucks and dumped like bright orange Easter eggs for the finding. Bales of hay pop up here and there, forming tiny mountain ranges across the mostly flat land.

Others wander the field. Even from this distance, I recognize the look on their faces. A combination of desperation and weariness. I saw the same one in my rearview mirror anytime I shot a glance at myself on the drive in. They notice my arrival, stop, and turn toward me, all arms in the air waving and pointing. What's all the fuss about? I can't make out their words, so I set one foot in the mud and enter the patch.

A scarecrow–lumpy and in a plaid button up and overalls–lazily points me onward. I nod in acknowledgement and travel deeper into the field, stepping as carefully as one might in a graveyard, the pumpkins deserving the same reverence as burial sites. Thick, grey vines web out across the dirt, like veins pumping life to distant limbs. I stand still and watch them pulse accordingly. A breeze hits my face and snaps me back to the reality in which I realize that's not how normal vines behave. I look up to a solid, pale-pewter sky for some relief, but find a storm forever rolling in, never quite arriving. Eyes back to the ground, I see a fingertip in the mud, bending, beckoning, using its nail to slowly dig out whatever's at the other end of it, and I decide it's time to leave. My body moves in the direction from which I arrived, but I make no headway toward the parking lot. It's eternally at the end of my vision, the row stretching into the distance, a journey with an unreachable end. My car is there as it should be, I can see it, but no amount of walking gets me any closer.

Yet I walk. I walk more. I watch pumpkins run through their entire life cycle, seeds to sprouts to plumping gourds to collapsing globes of mold and rot. How easily I could reach middle age here, go gray, lose my libido, my teeth, my mind. How easily I could die here and break down into particles small enough to mingle with the soil. I pull my phone from my jacket pocket. No signal; every call dropping as the rain threatens to.

"Hello?" I yell across the field, hoping someone's within earshot. "What's the way out?"

Several people look up, but only one, a man, waves and trudges toward me. His gaunt cheeks suggest a missed meal or more. Mud covers his body. He stops in front of me and bends, resting his hands on his knees to catch his breath. When he stands, it's hardly upright and my back aches looking at him. His eyes appear sad and wet from crying, yet his smile is warm.

"We tried to warn you."

"Warn me?"

"The field, once you set foot on the dirt of the patch, you can't leave unless you find your pumpkin. There's a pumpkin for everyone. You'll know yours when you see it."

He relays this dump of information so matter-of-factly, as though it's sensible and I'm meant to accept it without question.

"What?"

"I've seen many people come and some go. The ones that left all found a pumpkin. It's the only way out, I know it. I'm still looking."

"Why don't you just pick any one of them and leave?"

"It doesn't work that way. You can only take what's yours."

"I just want to get back to my car. I have a long drive ahead of me."

"Won't happen. You can waste your energy trying to escape or you can spend it focusing on the task at hand. I think it'll make sense in the end, why you're here. We all came looking for something. This place isn't an accident."

None of it makes sense, but I can't convince myself this starving man would stay here if he had some other option. Out of the corner of my eye, the digging finger has now exposed an arm up to the shoulder. The man notices my distracted gaze.

"You'll see worse than whatever it is over there that's caught your eye."

I opt to not discuss the finger and its arm specifically. "Is any of it real?" I inquire.

A woman screams in the distance as she flails her arms in front of her at something invisible to me. The man doesn't even look in her direction.

"As real as the burden they represent." He looks down at the soil and jumps a little. "I have to keep moving, the vines are coming."

Indeed they are. I look around us and they've all begun inching in our direction, promising to pull us under. I see marks on his jeans where the mud was rubbed away, the vines having caught up to him before. I watch him struggle back and return to his careful examination of each gourd in his path. The vines retreat when I too move again.

I begin my search in earnest for this talisman of power and purpose, this ticket out. Every pumpkin looks wrong to me. I'm not sure how it should look. Some appear identical, cloned from the same seed, mimics of some master pattern, placeholders for future prisoners of the patch. Hours pass, they must, but the sky remains a deep, angry grey and the light never changes. I can't imagine ending up stuck here in the dark, bumping into one another, tripping on gourds, not knowing if we've passed right by the one meant for us. For that reason alone, I am grateful for the unnatural, unending day. In the distance, the finger-turned-arm has become half a man struggling to claw out of the quicksand of his predicament.

A woman passes, counting to herself with clock-like regularity, tracking the day that doesn't track itself. I wish to know how many days she's been here, but fear any retribution for interrupting her log.

A hay bale of peculiar shape beckons me to rest. Its bulk and branches stick in all directions, suggesting it's more of a free form sculpture shaped my minds and hands than anything a programmed machine could ever spit out. At its size, it's a bit of a miracle I didn't see it from the road. I sit with respect for the art, away from its most delicate looking appendages, and halfheartedly glance around for a plaque declaring the title of the piece and the name of the behemoth's creator. I sit and moisture, expelled by the weight of my weary body, soaks through my pants. I'm so tired it doesn't bother me. I lean to one side and pull my feet up until my head rests on a bulkier part of the straw mass. It shouldn't be comfortable, but it feels like home.

Sleep takes me without consent or forewarning. The vines become my veins. My head is full of seeds. I cough dirt. I speak in crow. A fever dream within a waking nightmare.

"Hey! Wake up, man!" The unofficial patch attendant's voice pulls me back.

My eyes open and I'm human once again. Near the top of the structure, in a break of the course strands, I see a brush of black fibers sticking out like spider legs. They move up together and back down and I realize it's an eye, opening and closing. I stumble to my feet.

"Someone's in there!" I announce to the field at large, as though anyone has time or energy to care about something outside of their own search. Only the man is near and cares to come closer. His cheeks are caving in, like the rotting pumpkins from earlier.

"Yes, someone is in there," he confirms, "I see my son. And the thing you should know about him is that he committed suicide years ago. I'm guessing, if you look closer, this person is someone you know."

I lean in and pull some straw away from the face and see a recognizable beauty mark just below the left eye. One I can identify anyway. My heart drops.

"It's Samantha, my first girlfriend. Why is she here? How is that possible?"

"The same reason I see my son. Makes sense doesn't it? Stay still long enough, stop trying to survive, give up. That mindset consumes you. Here, the hay or the vines do instead."

"She died of an overdose when we were teens."

"My son shot himself in the head."

"Why is she here?"

"We can't let them go. We blame ourselves. This...this is a monument of unrest."

"She's still alive! I saw her eyelids move!"

"Your memory of her is alive."

He pulls a small knife from his pocket and, before I can stop him, deftly slices through a piece of hay down to her neck where life in large arteries lives. She shudders, but only dirt falls from the wound.

"She made her choice a long time ago. You can't save

her and you have to live with that. Sometimes, no amount of help is enough. If you want, you can lie back down and let the hay take you all the same. It nearly had you anyway, before I woke you up."

I look at my clothes and see the marks of dirty, snaking hay and vine.

"How do I stop seeing her? I still have nightmares. Sam showed up here! That means something!"

"Sit with her and say your peace, then turn your back to this monstrosity."

"But you said you still see your son?"

"It doesn't hurt as much as it did. He doesn't stare at me anymore. He blinks less often. Take what healing you can get. It'll never go away completely and remember, it gets worse here, or at least not any better. Find your pumpkin and get the hell out!"

I can tell my presence wears on him. My constant need for assistance cuts into his own progress. He seems so happy to help, even though he's disappearing to do it. Maybe I'm playing the part of one of his apparitions? Feeding off his overly helpful nature, keeping him from success. How many iterations of me have come in advance of my own arrival? It would suit him well if I got out of here soon.

I fall into a rhythm. Step, bend, look. Step, bend, look. The more I look, the more I begin to know what I'm not looking for, the easier it is to tell what isn't for me. Crows circle overhead and spin into larger, more ominous birds. Corvidae to Accipitridae. Near a far edge of the field, a man falls to his knees and the vultures drop to reap the harvest of his flesh. The vines inch closer and the sky and earth battle for a meal.

I search the field with new resolve as the roof of the barn opens up at its peak and a parade float-sized version of my father, hulking and mean, emerges like a jack-in-the-box from the framing. His giant eyes follow my every move. My cellphone chimes from my jacket pocket. There's still no signal, but message after message from my father come through. The notifications clog the screen causing the phone to freeze and shut down, yet the chiming doesn't stop.

"I'm never good enough!" My voice is tiny in comparison to his command. His level of scrutiny and displeasure overlooks the entirety of my life, within this patch, outside of it.

"There!" His voice is thunder from the stormy sky, causing my world to quake. He grins and points at a pumpkin in the distance. When I get to it, I know it's not for me, but he nods repeatedly, assuring me of his selection. I stand there for an eternity, trying to convince myself it's the right one, but no matter the angle of my approach, it never gains even a small bit of familiarity. He heckles every move I make, judging all failures like God himself. In fact, his giant hands settle in front of me to block my path down certain rows. I want to trust that he's helping, but increasingly it feels as though he's keeping me from where I'm trying to go.

"Leave me alone! I can do this myself!" I scream to the sky. He springs backward, like a punching bag clown and returns with full force in my direction, bobbing to and fro from the unexpected strength of my admonishment. I'm not watching where I'm walking and I run head on into a woman.

"Stay back!" she screams, though her wild eyes are

warning enough. "I've lost count!"

I realize it's the same woman from before, the walking clock. She's losing minutes over me. I take advantage of the few moments she'll allow me.

"Who do you see on the roof of the barn?" It's more of a demand than a question. I don't want to feel crazy alone. If someone will tell me their own story, maybe I can make sense of my own. The woman shakes her head. She won't look at the sky above the building. I grab her jaw in one hand and turn her face to the weather vane. My father there grins and eats some of the grey clouds floating around him like morbid cotton candy at this fucked up carnival show. He points at me more, as though I'm the main attraction. She squints her eyes closed and pulls her face out of my grasp, refusing to take in whatever monster of her own perches there. Mud smears her cheeks where my fingers were, giving her the appearance of a soldier prepped for combat against her own formidable adversaries. She hurries off before I can implore her further, spewing numbers at top speed to make up for lost time.

The man is near me again, the one with all the information about this place. He's dried out, dehydrated, and his clothes hang off of him. He's missing teeth. His eyes grow foggy.

"The thing on the roof," he says without looking at it, instead gesturing with a wild arm in the direction of the barn, "don't listen to it."

"Why didn't you tell me that sooner? I've been on its wild goose chase for God knows how long."

"God? I don't think God knows anything about this place. This seems more like the Devil's work."

"Shouldn't someone be stationed at the edge to keep

people out?"

"You know yourself it's impossible to get back to the end of the field once you're in it. And even if we could, we'd be losing time and risking being swallowed by the vines."

"You could have done something! Anything!"

"We did, remember? We yelled. We waved our arms."

Somehow I've been here so long, I've already forgotten those efforts.

"Could you have yelled louder? I couldn't understand your words."

"Would you have believed us if you had?"

I consider the question for a minute that doesn't truly pass, or passes in a moment so minutely elongated it stretches to an hour without notice.

He puts his hands on my shoulders and stares me dead in the eyes. "Some things need experiencing. This place would have gotten you on the dirt somehow. Ignore the thing on the roof. You're bigger than it."

His pep talk works and I find new focus. My father still hovers over my every decision. He's there, skulking in the corners of my vision, hemming and hawing about the paths I choose, but I'm able to ignore the bizarre noises coming from his cave-like mouth. Step, bend, look.

"Another!" someone screeches.

I look toward the lot and sure enough, a car has pulled in. I raise my arms to the sky and wave as others yell to the woman now exiting her vehicle. Even though we know it's hopeless, the urge is strong to warn her. She takes some level of notice, but, at the behest of the scarecrow, enters the field anyway. How much like her was I.

Step, bend, look, step, bend, look. The mud is up to my knees and there it is in the distance, my pumpkin. Still far, but within reach now that I can see it. I'm terrified to blink and find it rotted or rolling away.

"I found it!" I announce, a child on a scavenger hunt, eyes on the prize. "Finally!"

"Shhh," the man says, "the field will continue to distract you from your goal. Stay the course. Keep your head down. Some people spend their time here making sure others don't succeed. Pumpkin smashers."

I laugh. The man slaps my face. The crows pause mid-flight in wait for blood.

"It's not a joke. Don't let anyone near your pumpkin."

With a stinging cheek and wild glances in all directions, I approach the thing. I'd like to be offended by its general condition: bumpy, scarred, with many indentations marring its surface, but the more I look at it, the more of myself I see there. The more every angle finds it right and well with me. It's large, as though it went to seed when I was born and met each one of my growth spurts in kind. Growing here all this time I've been struggling out there, roughened up by those passing by on their own selfish journey of self-preservation. It's so large I'm not sure I can lift it, but the urge to embrace it overwhelms me.

I yank at the vine and this thing that should be mine grows thorns into my palms, resistant to the end, a greater battle than I anticipated. Blood seeps from the wounds and drips to the soil, which rises up with impatience to sip it. I hold tighter, turn and pull the umbilical cord until it snaps into a picture-perfect stem. With the life support cut, I survey the shape more closely to formulate a plan of movement.

"Lift with your knees!" someone yells. "Don't give up!" Encouragement they're only able to offer as they haven't yet found their mammoth, hard-rinded doppelgangers.

I set my core and heft it from the ground and we step over vines together, this newly harvested corpse and I. After only a few rows something catches me, and the gourd and I drop to the mud. It's a painful fall, with the bulk of the pumpkin crushing one of my arms. I'm unwilling to loosen my grip on the thing out of fear it might grow legs and walk away. At first I think I've snagged a vine, so I twist my ankle back and forth to free it, but whatever has me is holding, and holding tighter the more away from it I try to move.

Could it be a pumpkin smasher, bent on destroying my last hope for salvation? I pry free my trapped arm and look to my feet. A hand from the dirt holds me in place. I think of the unearthing finger earlier and shudder. I follow the painted fingernails, red as the perfect barn, down to their fingers wrapped around my pant leg. The hand turns and there is it, a wedding ring I recognize. The ring I gave to my wife.

Everything I've been avoiding is here. In driving away from it, I've run into it head on. Somehow it got out in front of me when I wasn't looking. I'm stuck in a corn maze without walls. Cornered in the rows by those closest and most damaging to me.

I struggle against her grasp. She refused to sign the divorce papers, pressured me into staying in the house I couldn't afford on my own. I tug, jerk my leg up and down. Her nails dig into the flesh of my ankle, her dissatisfaction sinks its teeth into me. Then I remember it, that one night over dinner when the words slipped out of my mouth.

"I haven't been happy in a long time."

I say it again, but differently.

"I'm not happy!"

Her grip loosens.

"I don't love you! Let me go!" I yell, owning my own disinterest, accepting my want to be free of the shackles she'd imposed here, at home, everywhere I turned.

She lets go. I leave her in the ground and my gourd and I find a way back to our feet. The cows no longer face South. They're staring at me, in whatever direction this is, wherever the fuck I am.

"What's with the fucking cows?" I yell, but my voice only hovers around me before dropping into the dirt.

"What cows?" croaks a woman's voice. I point to the once-grazers as I look up to where the voice originated and see a woman there on the scarecrow's perch, plaided and coveralled, pierced and bound, crucified, on watch over everything. She clutches a tiny pumpkin in one hand.

"Mom?"

I begin to think only of getting her down from her sacrificial cross and finding freedom together.

"Is that your pumpkin?"

She shakes her head and slips a shy finger from her grip to point at the one on the ground in front of us, still on the vine.

"That one's mine."

"Why are you carrying that one?"

"It's your father's. I'm protecting it from the crows."

"What about you, Mom? We need to get you out of here."

"What would you have me do, son?"

"Put his fucking pumpkin down before it's too late!"

The crows come then and I try to shoo them away, but they ignore me and start pecking at the softening flesh of her unclaimed gourd.

"I can't do it!" she screams as she watches them devour it. "I have to protect your father."

I look for a way to untie her, but the harder I pull, the deeper the cords cinch around her wrists and the more resolute she becomes in her position as mother, as knowing best, as a wife and a martyr for the happiness and safety of those she loves.

"Hey!" A hand grabs my shoulder and I turn to see the thin man there, barely there, an incredulous look on his disappearing face. "You're talking to a fucking effigy, man."

I look back to her, but he's right, my mother is gone and only the straw man hangs on the pole. I turn to where her pumpkin was and there her corpse lies, nearly picked clean and through by the still working beaks of the crows-become-vultures. I begin to move toward her, hating myself for letting things get this far gone. Within range, I see the vultures' true faces, greedy, selfish, and mustachioed like my father.

"Don't go to her, she isn't real. If you get any blood on you, they'll eat you too. They feast on weakness. Every ghost here does."

"Even the weird cows?"

"There aren't any cows."

Upon looking again, there aren't cows, but everyone left in the field is staring at my pumpkin and I, waiting for us to approach the edge that remains out of their reach. I look back one final time to thank him, but the gaunt man is now the scarecrow on the pole, worn to the semblance of a human. Maybe he was the scarecrow all along, guiding me to the center of my troubles. Maybe time can't be measured by clocks and daylight, but only in the hollowing cheeks of our caretakers, who spend so much time looking after us, they forget to live for themselves.

His straw finger points to the parking lot and I know I'll finally be able to leave. I expect applause when we cross the border, my burden and I, but there is only silent contemplation from those still stuck in limbo. Success is possible. My pumpkin and I are proof. My feet find the gravel of the lot, a welcome solid surface compared to the mud of the patch, and we make swift gains to my car.

I set my life in the front passenger's seat and strap the safety belt across its girth. Now that it's mine, I can't stand the thought of losing it. On the short trip around the car, I fear it might learn to drive and ditch me now that it's free. I pull the driver's side door closed and in that instant it's dark, as though the latch hit a switch to swap the sun out for the moon. For a moment I worry about the others still in the field, but somehow I know both the daylight and their search persist above the dirt. I check the rearview mirror for any sign of my gargantuan father, but there is only a red barn displaying dark burgundy in the dimness of the evening.

> *"FOR LIFE BE, AFTER ALL, ONLY A WAITIN' FOR SOMETHIN' ELSE THAN WHAT WE'RE DOIN'; AND DEATH BE ALL THAT WE CAN RIGHTLY DEPEND ON."*
> *- BRAM STOKER, DRACULA*

BECAUSE FATHER IS DYING

"I haven't seen you wear this dress lately."

That's what Mother first said, nothing about Father, only fabric. I examined its yellow print, faded and moth-eaten, unaware of the conversation I was entering by doing so. She knows how attached I get to things. She knows just how to trap me.

"I've always loved its color," I replied, attempting to justify keeping it, without letting on I understood her goal was otherwise.

"Do you still wear it?"

The question felt heavy, as though something bigger hinged on my answer to it. I could see wetness in her eyes from crying, something she usually kept to herself.

"No, but I admire the fabric sometimes, where it isn't yet ruined."

Mother pulled it from the closet. "You can love something, but if it's no longer useful you have to let it go."

"But there's still room for it in the closet. It's not bothering anything, just hanging there."

"It's one less thing to c-c-carry," she faltered as the tears returned.

"Carry where? What's wrong?"

"Your father isn't well."

"I know. He hasn't been well for a while."

Mother wrung my dress in her hands, her knuckles white with effort. "Yes, but it's more than that. He'll be on his way soon and there isn't room in the yard to bury him. I thought there might be, but I was wrong."

I went to the window to look out on the small plot and to hide my own tearing eyes, wettened by the thought of Father in the ground. The edges of the vegetable garden blurred. Her weeks of fretting over the asparagus and the fencing and the short distance between the two suddenly made sense. There wasn't even room for another seed. I looked at the graves to its side, where Grandfather and Grandmother lay. There wasn't room for another body.

"He's ours to bury and someday I'll be going too. If there isn't room for your father here, there isn't room for me."

"Please don't talk like that, Mother."

"It's better to be prepared than to avoid the inevitable. We need to move. We need to get rid of things."

"If I can't keep my yellow dress, what does Brother have to give up?"

"I haven't told him yet. Give me time."

"He loves his room. He won't want to leave it."

"A room can be anywhere."

"And Dog?"

"Dog will go wherever we go."

I knew Mother was right about that. Dog's head is full of rocks and his loyalty is as solid. She wiped her cheeks dry with the dress and went downstairs, leaving me to watch the empty hanger swaying on the rack.

I always thought she would die before Father, after two children and all of the laundry, all the dishes, she was bound to depart at the first chance her tired body was afforded. Where Mother is worn, Father is hardened, an ancient building, strong and reliable with age. But I look at him differently after Mother took my tattered dress. I study the deepening wrinkles on his face and the fading color of his skin and the closer I look at him, the more I see he is weakening in small, almost imperceptible ways as the years have gone. It seems recently whatever ails him has reached something integral, sending crumbling the cornerstone of his uprightness. His back is crooked and he is sunken and hollow in new places. He could be a day, an hour, a moment from complete collapse. I tiptoe around him, fearful that any quake or tremble will be enough to pull him toward the earth.

"Don't treat him like he's ill," Mother snaps at me for my carefulness. "Do things with him like he's well. We can prepare for what's coming, but we mustn't focus on it."

"What should we do?"

"Your most favorite things."

"He can't skip rope with me anymore. His knees are too weak."

"He can watch. He loves to see you happy."

Because Father is dying it's hard to be happy.

I ask him to braid my hair, something he has done from

the very moment it was long enough, since I was as small as Brother. Father used to pick me up and set me down in front of him, in front of the fire, but now I go to him already resting in his chair. I move backward until my shoulders touch his knees and even that minute pressure makes him inhale in pain.

"I think this is the last time," he tells me as he separates my hair into three equal bundles. He moves in slow motion, like he's teaching choreography to a new student taking notes on each step of a dance. Mother warned me this was coming, the end of even easy times together. She's been practicing the orchestration every night after Father has gone to bed, for after he goes away for good.

I watch the shadow cast on the wall by the flames, simpler versions of us and the complicated movements of his hands. I look for recognizable shapes, animals or faces in the silhouettes, but no matter how his gnarled, bony fingers twist and tuck, twirl and wrap, all I see is the sharp, quick movements of a spider.

"I haven't seen you in your yellow dress," he says as he ties off the bottom of the braid.

"What made you think of it?" I ask, but his head is turned toward the deep-amber fire and I know.

Because Father is dying he is giving away things as well, us and the farm, and everything eventually. He's already started letting go. Men come to do his chores that Brother is too young to manage. Men come to take away the tractor and the horses my Father no longer has the strength to mount or maintain. Father sends the men out to look for a new home for our family, one just like this one, but with a larger yard. It'll need three bedrooms. One for Mother, but it can be smaller since Father won't sleep with her any longer. One for Brother. One for me. We'll need a big kitchen, one where Mother may continue to cook the family meals, where Brother can roughhouse with Dog, and where I can do my school work at the big, wooden table that Father built, hand hewn and cobbled together from old pieces of barn timber.

It isn't long before they find the right farmhouse. It's not new at all, really. It's missing some siding and the garden is overgrown. A few of the windows need fixing. But it will be new to us and there will be enough room for Father to rest.

Mother spends hours sitting at our ancestors' graves, speaking to them about the upcoming journey.

"I know you're comfortable sleeping," she says into the dirt, into Grandmother's ear, "but it will be time to go soon."

When she speaks to Grandfather, it's directionless. She talks to the fields and the sky. He's been dead for a long time and doesn't hear through his body anymore.

I see her out my window, once again on the ground, talking quietly to the dead. My heart tightens in my chest and pushes tears out of my eyes. I don't want Father in the dirt, not here or anywhere. I prefer him above it where I can see him and he still talks to me.

"Sister, don't cry," Brother tells me from the doorway and Dog takes advantage of his distractedness to bite his hand. He smacks Dog in the jaw with the same bitten hand and they both whimper in brief pain.

"Brother, Dog, stop hurting one another."

Somehow Mother is already upstairs, summoned by

our juvenile chaos. "Children, get back to your lessons. Father expects big things from you and you won't have time for schoolwork during the dig. "I've let your Grandparents know we'll be leaving soon."

I've packed my clothes and books into my luggage. I can't help but notice there's room for one more dress. Brother decides to wear all of his clothes at once, but Mother tells him he can't dig if he can't move his arms and he won't make the long walk if he can't move his legs. Brother is lazy, so maybe that's his plan. He struggles to undress and packs his clothes as well.

Mother has more to gather up. The kitchen, the memories. But before the movers can take the pots and pans to the new house, she must make the elixir to wake our ancestors for the journey.

I look at the ancient recipe, determined to solve every curly letter of the script. *One cup of the blood of the dying.* A cup of Father's blood seems like more than he should spare. Mother sees my face as I scrutinize the measurement.

"He won't miss it," Mother says. "He'll make more."

She cuts his arm at the table, at the wrist according to a very specific diagram on the recipe card. He flinches, but only in his eyes. A petite stream, red like the Yule wreath's ribbon, seeps out of the gash and into the mixing bowl Mother has set beneath it.

"Get your Father a rag," she calls to me as she pulls a jar from one of the high cupboards. Dirt fills the glass. When I come back with the towel for Father, the dirt has been emptied into his blood and Mother holds a tiny vial of clear liquid over the reddened mud in the bowl.

One cup of the blood of the dying. A half-cup of dirt from the new yard. Two drops of a loved one's tears. Mother weeps when she thinks we're asleep. I've seen her. She must have collected them then.

There are no other diagrams, no more instructions beneath the ingredients other than to *mix well.* I flip over the card, but the back is blank.

"There's nothing more to it. Your Father's blood and my tears tell them how much time he has left, the dirt tells them where we're going. They'll wake up when it's time to walk and they'll take the road to the new house like they've always known the way. Take a turn mixing it. Get your brother to help you."

The next morning, Mother walks Father from his bed to the yard. "It's time, children," she says as they pass by us at breakfast. "Finish your food and come outside."

I think I can hear Father's bones creak, but it's just Brother fidgeting in his wooden chair, trying to give Dog his bacon.

In the yard, we stand across from Mother and Father, the bowl of the paste between them.

"This won't be easy or fun. You will see things you will never forget," Father says.

"As hard as this will be, you two are lucky," Mother adds. "Some children go their entire young lives without ever seeing a death march."

I don't feel lucky. I've never once wished I could see dead things, never once pondered spending hours hauling soil to come upon them. It'd be easier if we could leave the past behind, keep it where we put it. Then we wouldn't have to dig up the backyard. But, because Father is dying, we have to face everything to make sure he has a place to rest and our ancestors don't feel abandoned.

"It's good to remember the past," Mother says. "It's important to stare death in the face and know what's coming. For all of us."

"Will they look scary?" Brother wonders, a hint of glee in his eyes.

"Grandmother has always been beautiful and Grandfather should be mostly bones by now. There isn't much scary about bones, is there?"

"I can't wait to see them!" he cheers as he eagerly grabs a shovel. Sometimes Brother forgets he's lazy.

With his hand above the bandaged wrist, Father tells us where to dig. After only a few shovels of dirt, I feel my heart in my ears and sweat covers my body. Father doesn't help because he can't die just yet and digging takes more life than he has left. He needs to save his strength for the journey. We dig forever, at least into the afternoon when the sun is highest, taking a break only for sandwiches and lemonade. Father and Mother tell us stories about the people we are exhuming. Grandmother was famous for her baking. Grandfather always worked too much. I feel bad for a moment that we'll be asking him to wake, now that he's finally getting some rest.

The movers leave with our belongings. Brother and I look on, confused about the two small jars of dirt they've taken with them from the piles we've made.

"They'll move us in and dig the new graves for us," Mother explains, "and they'll dump the dirt out into the new holes so your grandparents know right where to end up. Now go ahead, let's see them!"

We open their simple burial boxes.

Grandmother was buried in her wedding attire. I've

seen pictures of the day when both she and the dress had more life. Now, they are both threadbare. Her ancient legs look like two branches of weathered birch, and her breasts no longer fill out the bodice. There are holes in the silk of her gown that sometimes line up with the holes in her skin, allowing me a view into her body. There's nothing in there really, but darkness and some bugs.

Mother tuts and fixes Father's collar. "Always seems a shame to put such beautiful things in the ground to rot. Children, apply the mixture to their faces."

I scoop a fingertip of paste and smear it on what's left of Grandmother's nose, running it along her nostrils and above her upper lip like smelling salts.

"Wake up," I whisper in her ear.

"Give Brother the bowl," Mother directs.

Brother takes it and climbs down into Grandfather's grave. Grandfather has definitely been a skeleton for a while. He died before I was born and that's been almost sixteen years now. His once best suit cascades in all directions, a waterfall of dark, shredded fabric sent this way and that by the rockiness of his bones underneath.

"Grandfather, it's time," Brother tells him as he drops globs of the mixture into each of his eye sockets.

"It might not happen immediately, children. They will know when it's time to wake up."

"I'll wait." Now that the digging is done, Mother is right, we're lucky to see this.

"I'll wait too," Brother says and I hit his arm for copying me, though I'm secretly grateful I won't be alone for their resurrection.

Dog whines to be let inside.

I lie on my stomach at the foot of her grave, watching Grandmother for any sign of life. Brother sits with his legs dangling into Grandfather's plot, making grass whistle. Mother and Father talk about their beloved vegetable garden, which we'll have to abandon other than a few harvested seeds.

I'm about to go inside when I notice movement in Grandmother's face. She wiggles her nose and smiles and stretches her neck and before I know it she's sitting up. She extends a gloved hand to me and I reach in to help her out of her grave. The glove slips a little and a tear appears in her dried skin.

"Careful, Grandmother," I say softly. "Take it slow."

Just as she stands up in the yard, Grandfather begins to move his fingers. He lifts and drops them in a wave like he's playing the piano or impatiently waiting on something.

I expected he'd make a lot of noise moving. Clattering and clacking, like dishes falling out of the cupboard, or dominoes taking one another out. All I hear as he climbs from his grave is the swishing of the fabric of his three-piece as it rubs against itself.

He stands next to his wife, but it's not a reunion of any kind. They don't interact, there is no embrace. Maybe if their eyes hadn't turned to jelly they might recognize one another. They line up shoulder-to-shoulder and face forward like soldiers, quietly reporting for the day's duties.

"Good, everyone's here now."

Mother produces two small bells from the pocket of the apron around her waist, wrapped in fabric to muffle their ringing. She hands one to both Brother and I.

"What are these for?" I ask, not knowing the ceremonial details.

"Take some twine and tie the bells to your wrists. They will keep back lingering spirits hoping to inhabit the bodies of your grandparents."

"Once we start, we can't stop," Father warns. "Are we ready?"

Dog barks and I suppose he speaks for all of us because the march begins while I'm still securing the bell to my wrist.

"Remember children, don't let them lose their things."

Father leads the procession and sets the pace. Like Grandfather, he wears his best suit, the one usually reserved for weddings and holidays and meetings with important people. Mother follows just behind him in case he needs help walking or stopping to relieve himself. The ancestors fill the middle. I carry Grandmother's veil so it doesn't drag in the dirt and pull her skull from her spine. Brother has rolled up the cuffs on Grandfather's pants so he doesn't trip and fall on his own outfit. Dog runs everywhere. Into the woods, up ahead, under our feet. The wolves make up the back. All hoping to catch a loose limb or to sneak a snap at one of us still alive to grow weary from the journey. The bells help keep them at a distance.

Not long down the road, in the woods above the fields, Grandfather's boney feet disappear into the mud and Brother struggles to pull them free. "Are you sure I can't carry him?" he calls ahead to Mother. "We'll never keep up."

"The dead must move themselves! It's part of the ritual! It always has been! We'll see you when you get there!" Mother yells back from the front of the line.

I want to stop and help, but Grandmother doesn't

slow so I lose sight of Grandfather and Brother. I yell at Dog to protect them.

We overtake my parents, who have paused at a stream that runs beneath a bridge in the road. Father sits on a rock, taking deep breaths of the evening air. The magic that compels Grandmother to move forward does not compel her to turn her head in greeting.

"What do I do?" I call back to Mother.

"Keep going. We'll catch up. Your Father just needs to rest a moment."

"But how will I know where to go?"

"Grandmother will take you there, just like I said."

"It's getting dark. What if she makes a mistake?"

"Only the living make mistakes! You'll know it when you see it! Look for the holes in the ground! She'll take you right to them!"

We find ourselves otherwise alone in the woods, separated from the rest of the cortege, just myself and the bride on a long walk down a rustic aisle, a country road turned coffin line. How strange we must look to the animals watching from the darkness. A corpse in a gown and a tired, dirt-covered girl following behind her, veil in sooty hands.

"What is death like?" I ask Grandmother to break the silence, but even the sound of my voice doesn't distract her from her trance or return her voice to her throat.

Her silence makes me feel something I've never felt before, at least not that I can remember. Brother has always been there, and Mother before he arrived, but right now I feel alone. It's a funny thing, what a presence it has, a hulking, heavy weight I can't help but feel. It's almost as though we are three on the path, Grandmother, loneliness, and I.

I look through the trees at the other farmhouses we pass. Families watch our black parade from the windows. I'd like to wave a hello, but I'm worried about letting go of Grandmother's veil, as though releasing my grip will send her disappearing up ahead in regained speed and a returned detachment from the living.

Eventually, we arrive, all of us. Each pair and Dog, still barking his head off at everything and anything, and eventually the wolves who didn't gain much for their bellies arrive too and circle the farmhouse for a while, bent on giving some nutritional value to their journey.

Fields stretch forever into the distance and Mother tells me they all belong to us thanks to the tractor and the horses. There's room enough for all of us here, when we die. We'll never have to move again, though I secretly hope we might, just so I can see Father once more. I'd happily dig him up, easily say goodbye to another to watch him move again. There's room enough for my grave and Brother's, if he decides to stay here. Maybe even for his wife and their children. We've already marked a spot for Mother to lie when death becomes her preference, right next to Father's. Someone has come before us to dig the holes and my aching arms are grateful.

Grandmother finds the small pile of dirt marking her grave and climbs in with a grace reserved for the living. Grandfather walks straight ahead into his grave, letting the ground disappear beneath him. He collapses into a pile of bones and fabric when he hits the bottom.

"I'll join you soon," Father tells them before going

inside to rest for a while. Mother follows after him.

Brother grabs a shovel. "When do we put in the dirt?"

"Not yet. We need to let the life run out of them. Then they will meet Father on the other side. That's what Mother told me anyway."

We keep watch over the open graves, our lives running slowly out of us. We ring our bells to keep the spirits, wolves, and other scavengers at bay. Grandmother settles in, shifts and turns until she's nestled into her place in the ground once more.

Grandfather's bones don't rest and I can see Brother getting nervous, playing with something small in his hand.

"What did you take?" I ask and he hides his hands behind his back. "Show me or I'll tell Mother!"

"It's just a toe, I think." He holds up the piece of bone and I grab it before he can snatch it away again, throwing it into the open grave with the rest of Grandfather, who calms immediately.

Brother and I bury them and talk about our long walks as we do, how Grandfather's toe came off in the mud and Brother collected it so the wolves wouldn't, how Grandmother seemed so full of energy even though the weight of her dress slowed her down. Father stands in the doorway of the farmhouse, listening to our laughter and the bells still dangling from our wrists.

Just as we pat down the last of the dirt topping our grandparents' graves, our parents come to join us at the remaining hole in the yard.

"I love you, but I need to lie down," Father says before kissing my forehead and hugging Brother. "Take care of your Mother. Be good to each other."

Mother holds him tightly and kisses and grips him frantically before helping him down into his new bed, made of pine and lined with velvet. He stares up at us and smiles and then closes his eyes as whatever long ago magic that brought him to life leaves his body. Men come and seal the coffin lid because Mother can't bear to do it herself.

"I'm sorry," she cries because Father has died. "I'm sorry."

The men shovel in the dirt, allowing Brother and I time to rest. Dog, a stick in his mouth, whines at our feet, demanding our attention.

> *"HE WHO FIGHTS WITH MONSTERS MIGHT TAKE*
> *CARE LEST HE THEREBY BECOME A MONSTER.*
> *AND WHEN YOU GAZE LONG INTO AN ABYSS THE*
> *ABYSS ALSO GAZES INTO YOU."*
> *- FRIEDRICH NIETZSCHE*

FIRESICK

Homestead

They wake and rise before the sun, being rearers of two boisterous children and several animals, and raisers of occasional crops, all of which demand ample and early tending. The man is the first to step outside, in case something wilder than their chickens wanders the yard. He is closest to his grunting and violent ancestors just after sleep and right before the memories of his dreams fade. When the silence greets him and not even the pigs shuffle nervously in the sharp morning air, he understands the area is safe. His feet find the path to the outhouse and his eyes remain closed as his mind enjoys the blissful delirium of having just woken up. Once inside and as he relieves himself of the rank urine that's waited hours to escape, he opens his eyes to the cool darkness. A spider's web clings to the wood of the corners in front of his face. He'll need to move her before she gives birth to many more. Maybe the barn, maybe in the rafters. She wouldn't be the first to see new life there. His wife bore his youngest, Charlotte, in one of the stalls when she refused to move once labor began.

The hinges of the outhouse door creak as he pushes it open.

Now that he is truly awake, he sees it. An opaque white in the air hugging every edge and corner of the farm, fastened to it like the spider's web, and perhaps awaiting the birth of something far worse. At first, he thinks it's fog, but then he smells it. Smoke. The memory of the path to home serves him as the smoke thickens. Inside the cabin, his wife makes breakfast. He stands in the doorway and calls to her.

"Alma, come see this."

She stands beside him, wiping the cracked bits of shell and viscous whites of broken eggs off her hands and onto an apron of her making, surveying the changed landscape. "I *thought* the air smelled different."

Josephine, the older of their two girls, joins them outside. "Mama, how will we take care of the animals?"

Alma seeks the small, pitched roof of the chicken coop in the distance where she knows it to be, but can't find its shape in the cloud. "By memory, I suppose. You can make a game of it. Finish your breakfast and get it done before things worsen."

"Paul, breakfast is ready."

After breakfast, Paul kisses his wife, leaving egg and bread from his beard on the smooth surface of her cheek.

"I'll try to chop wood for tonight," he says as he steps

out into the smoke again. On the side of the house, he feels for the grain of the axe handle and slides a hand down to the cool metal of its blade.

Alma listens to her daughters, who sing playful songs in the distance and call to one another off and on as they work toward completing their chores. When their voices grow farther apart from one another, she worries.

"Don't lose track of Charlotte!" she yells into the abyss, hoping Josie heeds her.

The sounds of cracking and splitting wood bounce off of distant, unseen objects. A bitter taste coats his tongue and specks of ash cling to the sweat building on his arms and forehead. *It will have to be enough*, he thinks. Gently, he tosses the axe toward the side of the house, where he hopes it's out of the way, and fills his arms with wood for the fireplace. It feels odd to plan for a fire when the air is already filled with smoke, but it's their only heat and light when the sun goes down.

He drops the wood before the fireplace and wipes his brow.

"You've smudged ash all over your face, Paul." Alma laughs as she wets a rag to clean him. "What do you think is burning?"

"Something big, that's for sure. Maybe a patch of the forest?"

"It's the driest summer we've had, so I wouldn't be surprised."

"I think I should check on the village. If we were burning, they would do the same for us. It's an awful lot of smoke."

Alma doesn't like the idea, but it isn't her place to

question her husband. His decisions were usually beneficial to her and the girls. To trust, that was part of their wedding vows.

As he prepares to leave, Alma worries about small things; how difficult the smoky smell is to remove. She recalls the hours spent scrubbing the girls' dresses after the bonfires of the Fall Festival and how the thick aroma clung to their hair for days. She thinks of bigger problems, like little Charlotte's lungs, already sensitive to some of the pollen in the spring and summer and how short of breath even running makes her. Alma remembers how the leaves on the trees had just started to change from their rich greens to their fiery oranges, yellows, and reds and how quickly it can happen, making skeletons of the trees, sun-bleached and bare. She fears the smoke will hang around the branches and rob her of the enjoyment of witnessing the turning.

The girls return from their blind expedition of feeding the animals. Alma brushes ash out of their hair. "This will all clear up when the rain returns."

"How soon is that mama?"

"Soon, I hope."

"Maybe today?"

Alma looks to the sky, or where it should be. Through the smoke, a bright orb shines without obstruction from clouds.

"No, but maybe tomorrow. Your father will get some answers."

"Stay inside. Don't breathe this for too long." Paul wears his daypack and a handkerchief around his neck. He holds

Alma close and then the girls.

"What about you?" Alma asks.

"I'll be fine. My lungs are hardier from the farm work. I'll wear this around my face."

She watches her husband disappear into the smoke as he heads for the forest path. The day passes slowly without any true sense of time through the smog.

When she feels like it's lunch time, Alma prepares porridge for the girls.

"It tastes burned!" Charlotte complains.

"It's not, that's just the smoke tricking us." Josie brings a hand up and pinches her nose. "Plug it while you eat!"

The girls laugh and Alma smiles, though she worries about her husband.

The Woods

Paul moves in measured footsteps, looking down and to his left for the larger rocks marking the edge of the path. It's not a safe way to travel, with one's head in the ground, but the smoke is so thick in the woods that he cannot see the trees in the distance, his hands when held in front of his face, or the many people he can hear traveling in the opposite direction who walk all around him both on and off of the path.

A cow passes near him, anxious and quick. His own cow was nervous from birth so he knows the right voice to use to speak to it. It approaches him and he can see the wounds covering its body. It breathes in ragged breaths. There are holes in its hide made with fire, charred at the edges. Some are bloody and others are clean and open into the hollow space between its ribcage and its spine. Paul reaches out to touch the cow and it runs away into the smoke.

A woman runs into him, nearly knocking him over. She does not apologize. Instead she picks up the things she dropped, a breadbasket, a bundled blanket, and a small stuffed animal, perhaps a child's toy. Everything is smudged black with ash.

"Are you all right?" Paul offers a hand to help her up.

She finally realizes he stands there before her. "No! It's all gone! Everything! They burned it all down!" She scrambles to pick up her belongings.

"Slow down! Who are they?"

"They are everywhere, all around us, coming for us. Don't speak to them. Don't let them in."

"Do you know them? Are they from the village?"

The woman looks around, fear contorting her face in all directions. "They *are* the village!"

"Tell me more. What happened?"

"Run! Hide while you can!"

The woman scampers off in the direction of the cow. Paul presses on with growing concern for Alma and the girls.

Homestead

Alma mends clothes with Josie and Charlotte, showing them stitches she learned when she was young. The smoke obscuring their world outside the walls is an easy excuse to catch up on things within their home.

"I'm making a proper mask for papa!" Josie showcases her double thick handkerchief.

"Me too!" The younger girl mimics her sister's hand motions, but her fingers are too small for such delicate work and all she holds is a scrap of thin fabric, unsuitable for anything helpful.

Outside, the chickens start up.

"Papa!" the younger girl screams as she runs to open the cabin door.

"Charlotte, no! He hasn't been gone long enough." Alma pulls her daughter's hands from the door. "It's something else."

"What is it, mama?" Josie asks, hiding safely behind her.

"A smoke monster," Charlotte squeals as she ducks under the large table in front of the fireplace.

"No, it's a man. He's whistling." Alma presses her ear against the door.

Charlotte purses her lips together but only a 'ptttthhh' slips out. "Is it a song we know?"

"You can't even whistle!"

"Maybe he can teach me?"

"Stay here, girls and stay out of view."

Outside the smoke has thickened. Alma's eyes widen as flakes of ash drift by, some of them clinging to the lace of her dress. She can tell a man approaches, by a darkness in the air in front of her and by the air pushing through lips in masculine melody, unconcerned of the mess he's inhaling to make the music. The sun could be shining, for all the glee that fills him, and maybe it still is, somewhere high above the smoke.

"Sir? May I help you?" She steps backward toward the house when he doesn't reply, but his whistling continues and grows louder.

"Oh!" Alma gasps, for the man is suddenly in front of her now, fully visible, emerged from the smoke and revealed. Burns cover his arms and black ash darkens his hands and face. Still he whistles.

"Hello, ma'am." The flesh of his burned lips fights to part as he finally speaks. The raw skin breaks open and bleeds as he smiles.

"You need help for those wounds!"

A chuckle rattles from his smoke-clouded chest. "I'm fine, really. It's no matter."

"But sir, you're bleeding. There must be something I can do."

Again he smiles without regard for the state of his lips and any further damage he may be causing. "Yes, there is, actually. Might I sit inside by the hearth to warm myself?"

From the door of their modest home, Charlotte's petite scream pierces the faux fog.

"Monster! Get away from my mama!"

Behind her, Josephine grabs Charlotte and stifles her own shriek.

"Please, forgive them. They don't know what they see."

"If you let me inside, I have something I'd like to show you all." The man steps closer to the front door, where her children still stand, staring.

Alma thinks of the safety her husband provides and how it's far away through the woods. "I can't let you inside. My husband isn't well. He's resting. I won't expose you to what he has. But you can stay in the barn. I'll bring you something to eat and clean dressings for your wounds."

Without touching him, she guides him around the house toward the barn, keeping him in sight.

"There's plenty of hay if you wish to make a bed. I'll bring you some milk and bread and something for your injuries." The scaly skin of his burned arm brushes against her flawless flesh and the roughness nearly makes her sick.

The man looks out from the barn at her. "That thing I'd like to share with you, I can show you in here just as well. Come."

"No, I'm sorry. I must mind the girls and tend to my husband. I'll be back soon." She rushes to the safety of her home and locks the door behind her.

The Town

Paul travels for most of the day, though he is unaware of the passing of time or daylight until sunset, when the smoke takes on a grimacing blackness. The village presents itself first to his nose. Acrid and thick, melted and still burning in places. Then, through the denseness of the air, patches of red and orange begin to dot the path. He enters through a large opening in the ivy-covered border wall. The ground transitions from dirt to a patchwork cobblestone, worn from use. It's a welcome change for his feet. The stone is darker than usual due to a thick coating of soot over its surface.

"Hello?" His voice hits the wall of smoke and disappears through the veil, traveling forever in a forward direction, unobstructed, echoless; no villagers reply. In the darkness, no work can be done to search for survivors. Paul shelters in a stone corner of the charred ruins of a church, beneath what remains of the wooden roof. He and Alma don't believe in the god that was worshipped in the space when it was whole. He wonders what god would allow such destruction anyway. The night passes at an aching pace, and he turns on the dirt with each crumbling sound of the destroyed village.

Cold jolts him awake, and he slaps the dewy stone wall of the pointless sanctuary with a hand gone numb. Where eventually the rain will wet the dirt, he urinates. The ashes of a burned down cross scatter the ground.

In the light of the day, and now that the fires have slowed and the smoke has dissipated, he can see the true scope of the damage. Thirty structures reduced to charred skeletons. Where barns and homes once stood, only black, crooked and distorted monuments remain. The village is a morbid cemetery, with no headstones to leave flowers.

He walks sometimes on the roads and other times on paths between the buildings. He explores the ruins, looking for signs of life. Instead he discovers the small bodies of children and the larger carcasses of livestock, all with lives stolen by flame.

Just as he resigns hope of finding anyone alive, a child speaks to him from behind a tree.

"Who are you?" she cries. "Why have you come here? There's nothing left to burn!"

Paul approaches her with caution. "I live in a house beyond the woods. I followed the smoke to see what was wrong."

"Did you meet anyone along the path in the forest?"

He thinks it an odd question, but decides a truthful answer is best, all things considered. "A woman fleeing from this, but no one else. Some traveled in the distance, beyond where I could see them. There was a cow. It was badly burned."

"And you haven't stared into the flames?"

"It was too smoky to see last night. Today I've looked all around, but the fire has died out. It's mostly ashes now.

What happened here? Where did everyone go?"

The girl puts an arm out, feeling in the air, trying to find him.

"You're blind? Did they do this to you?" He takes her hand and examines her exposed skin for trauma. One of her hands is raw and red. Still she uses it to feel his skin, with more zeal, as though he's hiding burns for her to find.

"No, I've always been blind. It's what saved me."

"I don't understand what happened."

"Come with me. I'll tell you."

She guides him back into the center of the village, beyond the tavern and the church he slept in, stepping carefully and avoiding the structures as she walks.

"Memories have weight. If I let my mind rebuild the walls, I feel the village as it was and it's easy to find my way. The road still rises the same, even though I know everything it leads to is gone."

He follows, impressed by her knowledge of the world she can't see.

The girl takes her time deciding where to tell her story. "Sit there." She picks a spot on the ground, soot-covered and featureless otherwise, no different from any area around it. Paul obliges, aware that a serious child shouldn't be questioned. She sits across from him and places her burned hand under her shirt. Sensing his discomfort, she explains, "my belly is cool. It helps the pain."

"Tell me what happened here."

"A stranger came into our village two days ago. She was covered in ash, nearly naked and with no belongings. She was badly burned. That is what the other children told me. They called her the scary lady. But the adults weren't fearful. They visited her and offered her food and clothing.

She had lost everything in a fire."

"How terrible." Paul shudders and shifts his body, sending tufts of ash back into the air.

"But something wasn't right about her," the child continues, "I knew this when my mother and father returned home after bringing her a portion of our supper. All they could talk about was the fire."

"The fire the woman survived?"

"No, the fire in our fireplace; how beautiful the flames were and how they wished that I could see it. I felt the heat growing. I knew then that the wall was burning." The blind girl points to her right and Paul realizes they are sitting in what is left of her home, not a randomly selected location.

"Why would they do such a thing?"

"I asked them, but they didn't reply. They left after starting it."

"They left you alone in the fire?"

"Yes. I burned my hand trying to find the door. I ran into the street and I could smell the other fires, hear them roaring as they grew. Yet no one screamed for very long. I guess because they looked into the flames and they got firesick too."

"What happened to the other children?"

"I don't know. Silence came quickly, once everything was aflame. It was too dangerous to search with my hands. Everything was hot and falling apart. I called out to my friends, but no one called back to me."

Paul can't bring himself to tell her they'd all perished, that he'd seen their bodies in the other homes. "And where have the older people gone?"

"They just left. They set the town on fire and walked away. At least that's what I think."

Wolves howl and whine in the distance. Paul imagines a great herd of them arriving to scavenge through the ash for the bodies of the children and animals.

"It's not safe here," the child cries.

"I can protect you from the wolves." Paul is already on his feet.

"Not the wolves, the people. They'll come back. You need to leave before they find you."

"Alma and the girls. They might have already reached them"

"You must go to them. Now!"

"What about you?"

"There's nothing here for me. My parents did everything."

"It's true, you wouldn't survive very long. It's a wasteland. What is your name?"

"Louisa."

"Louisa. My name is Paul. I'll bring you back to our farm. But we must be careful."

Homestead

Alma wakes in the middle of the night, coughing on the thickness of the air, forced from her sleep by a nightmare, one in which the smoke had finally cleared only to reveal a newly barren land. Everything she knew had been carried away with it.

The girls attempt their morning chores while Alma begins making breakfast, but shortly after they leave to find their way through the smoke, Charlotte comes back inside, crying.

"I can't find the chickens."

"If your papa can find the outhouse with his eyes

closed, I think you have it in you to find the coop in all this smoke."

"I found the chicken's house, but the chickens aren't there."

Josie returns looking more defeated than her younger sister. "The pigs have run off. I dumped their food in the trough. Maybe they'll come back for it."

The smoke is frightening enough to them, Alma can't imagine how confused the animals must be.

"I'm going to check on the cow in the pasture. Josephine, stay with Charlotte. Don't leave the cabin."

Alma brings a nearly empty bag of feed with her as she heads in the direction of the field.

"Gracie!" She calls for the milk cow until her throat is hoarse. Without their animals, they won't stave off hunger for long. Eventually, animals do come to eat, drawn to her loving voice carrying through the smoke, but the animals do not belong to her family and many of them are badly burned. She shoos them away and walks back toward the cabin.

A creature emerges from the woods. Alma can't place its name, as it seems to be missing parts. It nears and its true identity is revealed. The horse, now without tail or mane and missing one of its ears, approaches with fearful caution, but just as Alma strokes it's muzzle, two dogs cut across the yard, biting at one another, growling, and licking their raw wounds.

The Woods
"Listen," Louisa says from Paul's shoulders.

"I don't hear anything."

"You have to try harder. Get the smoke out of your head." She sticks wet fingers into both his ears, which he pulls out.

"Hey! Why'd you do that?" He uses what his daughters' call his 'papa voice' to scold the girl, before realizing he can now hear everything better. "Uh, thank you."

"I think there are people out there." Louisa's legs squeeze tighter.

"These woods are filled with boar and turkey. Now that the smoke is letting up a little, they're coming out from hiding and going back to their wandering around."

"Animals don't speak. Listen!" She cups her hands around Paul's ears.

Paul slows his pace and turns his head. Voices drift onto the path.

"It was magnificent!" a man recounts.

"I know. We must show everyone!" a woman's voice replies, sounding nearer.

Through the smoke, Paul makes out tall, dark objects he believes are trees, but some of them begin moving toward the girl and him.

"Don't come any closer," he yells as they advance. "I have a weapon!"

"Do you?" Louisa asks.

"Yes," he whispers, "a gun."

"You might have to shoot them. They're crazy."

"It's okay," one of the voices soothes, "we have something wonderful to show you."

Another speaks up. "You should leave this girl. She cannot glimpse the beauty of the new world."

"What are you saying? This child lost her entire village." Paul replies, holding Louisa close to him.

"I know this woman by her voice," Louisa whispers. "She is from my town. She is Kino, the baker."

"Why did you burn your homes?" Paul asks. "What happened to the children?"

The woman steps closer, nearly visible. "Our families will always be with us in our hearts. We can see them when we watch the flame. Would you like to meet our little ones?"

The people descend on Paul and the child from all directions, out of the smoke. They are no longer soft and dry, nor colored in creams and pinks. They are scabs, wet with puss, and black, and red.

"No! I must get home to my family!"

"Yes, we'll come with you," they all offer at once. Fifteen people suffering various injuries move closer. Paul can smell their putrid flesh.

"Seek a doctor! Your burns are festering!"

"You can help us. Sit us by the fire. Let us warm our bodies."

Anger begins boiling in Paul's stomach, anger towards the people who seem more blind than Louisa. "Fire has done this to you! Why would you want to be near it again?"

"Let us show you!" They move to surround him and begin to touch his arms and Louisa's legs.

"Stay away from us! Let us go!" Louisa screams as she kicks her legs.

Paul watches as trees around them go up in a newly kindled flame.

"Don't look at the fire!" Louisa screams at him. "Close your eyes if they try to show you!"

Paul slips from their hands, away from the growing flames, and runs down the path as fast as he can. Louisa bounces on his shoulders, feeling heavier with every step.

The strange people don't run after them, but he knows they'll catch up eventually. The path only leads to his farm.

Homestead

Earlier that morning, back on the farm, Josephine finds her mother sitting up in bed, reading the farmer's almanac.

"Mama?"

"Yes?"

"Charlotte's not in bed."

Alma feels around in her own bed, but her younger daughter isn't there either, as she sometimes ends up. "Did you look under it?"

"Yes. She wasn't there."

Normally, Charlotte's absence wouldn't alarm Alma, but with the strange man in the barn, the missing animals, and the smoke in the air she's uneasy, especially with Paul still away. She leaves the warmth of her bed and trades the comfort for a thin robe. Together with Josie, she checks the rest of the house. In the main room, a fine powder covers the floor. Near the door, the outline of two tiny feet, stand frozen in time in the ash. The toes are unmistakable as Charlotte's. Alma prays silently that she will find her child, that Charlotte hasn't disappeared like the animals. She opens the door and more ash swirls inside.

"Charlotte! Charlotte, where are you?"

"Charlotte!" Josephine screams.

"Josie, check the barn!"

As her older daughter disappears around the back of the cabin, Alma runs to the field, reckless in her footing, stomping through the muck of dead and dying things, scanning for her daughter's nightgown and fair skin.

"Charlotte, come out right now!" Alma cries. The

tears steal her vision. Someone touches her arm.

"Hello, ma'am," a woman greets. The voice is unfamiliar, but the words she's heard before.

"What are you doing in our field? Have you seen a little girl?" Alma wipes the tears away and takes in the sight of the woman. She is grotesque, a walking corpse, her skin and muscle burned away to the bone in some places. Her wounds are far worse than the man's, but she doesn't appear to be in pain. Instead, the woman is calm and friendly.

"May I come inside and sit by the fire?" The voice escapes the stranger's body, but there are so many holes in the woman's face where flame has eaten her, that Alma can't place the woman's mouth.

Before Alma can reply, Josie reaches her. "Mama, the barn's on fire!"

"Come, let me show you something," the woman whispers as she grabs Alma's arm and pulls her towards the woods across the field, away from the burning barn and her children.

"Go back inside and wait for me, Josie! Don't let anyone in!" Alma pulls her arm free of the woman's grasp and runs back in the direction of the cabin and the barn. Above the cabin, she can see the reddish orange of giant flames.

"It's magnificent!" the woman shouts from behind her.

Alma runs to the barn, along what she thinks is a clear path, until the prongs of a garden rake puncture her left foot. Already blind from the smoke and ash, made worse from the fire of the barn, she doesn't allow the pain to slow her. She limps, blood dripping into earth, bloody handprints decorating the skirt of her dress, to the fiery destruction. When she arrives at the barn, Josephine is there, staring at it as it burns.

"I told you to go inside! Go!" She watches her older daughter disappear behind the house.

"Charlotte! Are you in there?" Alma listens for a reply, for screaming, for anything.

"Hello, ma'am."

The words weaken her. They mean nothing good.

She turns at the familiar voice of the burned man. "It was you! What have you done with my daughter? Where is she?" Alma wishes she'd grabbed the rake instead of stepping on it, or the axe, wherever Paul left it in the haze.

"She's in the barn, ma'am. Gone, like the animals."

"No…"

Alma rushes through the flames and finds temporary safety beyond the rafter supporting the door. Charlotte's small form is visible, lying in the hay of a stall, her legs poking out beyond the door. Her skin is black and charred, her nightgown burned away. Alma tries to go to her, every bit of her aches to be with her child, but the heat is too intense and her body shies away from the flame.

Josephine still lives, Alma reminds herself through the pain, *I must stay alive for her*. She emerges from the barn and finds the burned man, who still watches the destruction, wide-eyed and smiling.

"How could you do this to my child?"

"Oh, no, I didn't do this. She started this fire herself. She crawled into it." He speaks matter-of-factly, with no sadness, as though it excuses the death of her youngest.

"She's a little girl! She doesn't know how to build a fire!"

"I taught her. Come, let me show you something."
The man extends a hand in offering, but Alma refuses to
take it. New burns overlap his older ones.

"Leave this place! Don't come near us again!"

"Josie!" Alma bursts through the front door of the cabin
and scans the living room for her elder daughter, who she
finds crawling toward a fire now blazing in the fireplace.

"Stop!" Alma screams as she dives onto her daughter.
"What are you doing? What has he done to you?" Josephine
keeps her eyes to the fire and Alma can feel her daughter
tugging away toward it again.

"It's beautiful, Mother. Let me show you."

The heat of the fire dries the tears on Alma's face as
soon as they roll over her skin. "I don't want to see any
more fire, Josie. It took your sister. It may have taken your
father."

Josie laughs at the suggestion. "But Mother, look!"
She points a finger into the center of the flame and lets the
fire eat at the flesh of her hand. "Charlotte is there!"

"What's gotten into you?" Alma cries as she pulls Josie
back once more. She raises her eyes from the burns on her
daughter's hands to the dancing flames in front of them
and something catches her eye. Beyond the oranges and
yellows, a familiarity sits, a feeling of comfort and home
that Alma has searched for her entire life. It's more than
even Paul and the girls have given to her soul. "We should
put some on the table, so we can sit with it," Alma suggests.

"Oh Mother, that's a wonderful idea!" Josephine hops
to her feet and runs to take her seat at the large table in the
center of the room, eager for the coming conflagration.

Alma grabs log after burning log with bare hands and

stacks them on the table in front of her daughter. The flames light up her child's face as they eat at the wood of the table and the delicate offering of her firstborn's flesh.

Paul and Louisa near the edge of the wood where, against all reasoning, the smoke is thicker. Ahead, blocking his way on the path, a small, dark mountain rises from the dirt. The mound reeks of charred flesh and hay.

"What on Earth?"

"What is it?"

"It's my animals, the chickens, our milk cow, the pigs. They're dead, burned, and left here on the path."

"The sickness beat us here. We're too late."

He steps around the carcasses of his farm animals and takes Louisa off his shoulders. She smells the air.

"Things are burning."

"It's everything, Louisa. It's all gone."

"And your family?"

"I don't know. I don't know! Alma? Girls?" He yells as loud as his smoke-dried throat will allow.

He finds the outhouse still standing, untouched by any flame, a solitary beacon of hope surrounded by the cremated remains of his life. The girls could all fit inside, if they'd had time to hide from the arsonists, the firesick. He opens the door and sees that the smoke has crept through the vents and filled the airspace down to the hole in the ground. His hands grasp into the smoky darkness and find nothing to grab ahold of but the spider and her empty web.

He walks from the outhouse to where the cabin should be, but little remains beyond the stone fireplace. The front door is a pile of ash to step over. To his right, a bent and burned body lies on the floor where the table once was. The size and shape are unrecognizable, save for the one remaining foot he discovers beneath the soot and the scar that runs along its top, an injury Josephine sustained as a toddler.

"Oh, my Josie!" he wails as he scoops her up however he can. His hands collapse through her flesh turned black by the flames. He looks through the burned out walls to the barn, where things still burn.

"Alma! Charlotte!"

In the barn, his heart dies more. Charlotte lies lifeless and burned in the stall where she was born. He runs to her and scoops her up the same as his eldest, but no life remains. Paul remembers another child, left alone in the middle of his loss. His kisses Charlotte on her cheek, reeling at the scent and sets her gently back to the earth. He leaves and finds Louisa crouching near the outhouse, quiet and still.

"I'm sorry I left you," he cries. "I'm so sorry I left."

And Louisa knows he isn't even talking to her.

"I have to find your mother."

Paul stumbles through the funeral pyre of his farm. He stands in the field, amongst the dead animals and dying crops. For a moment the smoke clears and he can see her, a woman, standing at the far edge of the field. She wears Alma's nightgown, smeared with ash and blood. Her arms are burned from playing with fire, but her face is not pained over the wounds or the loss of her children or the farm. Someone stands near her, hairless and crisp, wavering on their feet, nude but nearly formless. The horrible beast whistles a beautiful song that cuts the cloak of the air and climbs into Paul's ear.

He brings his hands to his face, smearing the remains of his daughters on his cheeks as he cups them around his mouth to ensure his voice will travel over the field.

"Alma!" he calls and she turns to look at him, drawn to the voice of something loving, just as the strange animals had been drawn to her.

"She's alive?" Louisa asks, placing a hand on Paul's arm, both to comfort and to warn.

"Yes, but she's not right."

"Don't call to her. We need to hide."

Paul hears the girl, but his concern lies with his wife. Maybe he can help her. "Alma, what happened?" he screams. "Where are you going?"

"There's nothing left for her to burn," Louisa replies.

"Who's that with you?" Paul cries as he drops to his knees.

"It's another ember," Louisa answers, though she cannot see, "to spread this fiery scourge."

Alma smiles and runs toward them, her damaged arms reaching out in welcome. She doesn't care that her husband and the safety of him have returned to this place. She can't remember his name. Her eyes are wide, alight with a wild energy he has never seen and though Paul wants to, he can't look away.

"Come here!" she yells, nearly upon him. "I have something wonderful to show you!"

"SOON YOU WILL HAVE FORGOTTEN ALL THINGS:
SOON ALL THINGS WILL HAVE FORGOTTEN YOU."
- MARCUS AURELIUS, MEDITATIONS

LAST CALL

"I mean, you said you didn't want it anyway, remember?"
Lauren tries to find a silver lining in the dim lighting of the
bar. Out of the corner of my eye, I see the glow of dying
candles set on nearby tables glinting off dusty, years-old
Christmas tinsel hanging sadly above her, outside of her
vision.

I lift my head, heavy and warm from the whiskey she's
been pouring. "Hmmm?"

"It's another 'no', isn't it? You haven't touched your
Guinness and you didn't decline the bourbon. Bourbon is
always for bad news with you."

I'd opened the envelope half a bottle of Maker's
earlier, thinking there was good news inside, one of those
rare correspondences, something worth struggling with a
champagne cork over. It had that kind of weight to the
paper anyway. Lauren watched me read it and saw me close
up and fold in on myself over another failure. I didn't
bother reading beyond the first line. It never made sense

to me why they waste ink on empty words when a plain, simple 'NO' typed center in the page wouldn't hurt any differently.

"They didn't even spell my name right."

She'd slowly pulled away the unopened champagne, like lowering the gun of a good time whose bullets I'd no longer earned. The thick, rectangular glass of the whiskey bottle replaced it in my immediate vision and she's right, I didn't reject the amber-hued offering. She knows just how to comfort without laying a finger on me, but I'd have thought she'd know by now these letters I receive are never a cause for bubbly.

The rye and spice burn my throat, a tolerable pain I've asked for, one I can control. I set the tumbler on top of the rejection letter and let the sheet take up the job of a coaster. The condensation from the glass seeps into the dry paper, a slow rising tidewater that begins to blur my shortcomings; a preamble to the whiskey's full effect. The ink stretches out, yawns and reaches. Maybe I can coax the letters into another, more acceptable shape, an A+ instead of an F. I will it into a better grade with my mind.

"Fuck them." Lauren pulls the paper off the bar before I can decipher it's new messages, crumples it and tosses it overhand into an overflowing trash bin at the end of the tabletop. It's at home in the garbage with the red cocktail straws and the sliced lemons, the fruit flies.

I grab the whiskey and pour myself another. Lauren doesn't try to stop me.

"It's not like you're not getting jobs! You've had plenty of callbacks. I've seen your costume closet!"

"Yeah, full of neck-to-floor sacks for evil witches in children's plays, high-waisted, elastic-banded pants for bloated woman twice my age in commercials about constipation, and shapeless gatherings of cloth for genderless, alcoholic bums in low-budget movies by no-name directors! Why am I always cast as an alcoholic?"

"The typecasting is real, Koryn."

"Hey! I've been cutting back!"

"Cutting back, huh?" She shows me the bottle and the small, sloshing puddle of ninety proof at its bottom, one hundred percent proof of my highly-skilled insobriety. "I guess there's still *some* left."

I feign a laugh. "All this rejection is starting to make me feel washed up before I'm even given the chance to make it. I'm a has-been who has *never* been."

"You just haven't found the right role yet. This happens to everyone, trust me. I've seen plenty of actresses come through here and not one of them had it easy. It's like climbing a ladder with Crisco-slathered rungs and cramping hands. You're going to fall. The whole system is built for you to fail."

"Then how do I succeed?"

"Honestly? Stop trying to climb the ladder and look for an escalator."

I hear her, but I'm too transfixed to reply. A vision from God-or maybe Bacchus, with the amount of alcohol in my system-appears on the television behind Lauren's head. The angelic face of a woman, her blonde hair glowing like a halo, graces the screen. I've seen her before, but never in this context, never as an answer to my troubles. I look away from the TV long enough to catch Lauren raising her eyebrows suggestively.

"See something you like?"

"I'm not like that."

"That's what you say, but every time they show that woman—what's her name?"

"Sandi."

"Yes, every time Sandi comes on you all but drool and today you're practically mesmerized. I'm just saying I've never seen you look at a *man* like that."

"I bet she could get any role she wanted. Whatever it is that makes some people special, Sandi has it."

"I don't see it," Lauren says. Maybe it's your beer goggles. You're always drunk when you're looking at her."

Up until a few months ago, when Sandi Brook made it big and started showing up on television, I had no specific idea of what constituted a perfect girl, no insight into the formula, only a few ingredients and some minor speculations from my uneducated viewpoint. I hadn't given it much thought except to know I definitely wasn't that woman in any areas of my life. I'm not skinny or sexy. My eyes are sooner described as 'poop brown' than 'chestnut' or 'autumn leaf'. I'm in debt. I have no style. But then I saw Sandi and knew for certain I was looking at a goddess, a stunning visage with a slim frame and winning smile all perfectly wrapped up into a bundle of eventual success at whatever she chose to pursue. Her face turns heads and silences rooms. What an incredible feeling it must be to be wanted by so many. Drinks paid for, doors opening left and right on your career path, everyone wanting a piece of you, the entire country buzzing your name.

To be fair, there is *some* buzz around my name. I was declared 'Most Likely to Become an Alcoholic' in my high school yearbook and at every reunion since, the open bar has been my chance to live up to that elected title. I'm dependably drunk most days, and I'm such a loyal customer at her bar that Lauren pours my Guinness before I arrive.

She slides my card over the countertop without a receipt, code for declined, code for 'try another'. I fumble through my wallet, a desolate wasteland of bad credit and high interest rates, examining the rectangle plastics for something with less wear, a newer model that won't break down on the highway. I'm grateful for her discretion and show it with a scribbled tip I can't afford. I just need one audition to pan out, one gig to pay up and I can begin to dig out of the hole in which I've put myself.

"Are you sure you're okay to drive?" Lauren asks as she always does, a contractual obligation, even though she knows down to the milliliter exactly how much I've had to drink, which is definitely above the legal limit.

I can't imagine abandoning my car in the lot overnight, coming back to claim it tomorrow with the hangover I'm guaranteed to be nursing, so I give her a thumbs up and lose my balance, glancing around the bar to make sure I didn't gain an audience for the wrong reason.

"Koryn, I can call you a cab. It's no problem," my dealer tells me, earlier a sinner, now a saint.

"I'm fine. I'm functioning!" I declare, though the world spins a bit. I use the leftward drag of my vision to help get me out the door.

In the lot I let the engine of my car idle as I sober up a little and hatch a plan, one I hope I have the guts to follow through with tomorrow when I can see straight.

The next morning, my agent calls before my queasy stomach forces me from bed. I let him leave a voicemail and listen to the recording with my eyes closed. I've received so many from Ari just like it.

"I heard about that last casting call. I'm sorry it wasn't the right fit."

Usually I curl up and cry. Today I sit up and call him back. It only rings once before he answers.

"You never return my calls! To what do I owe this privilege?"

"I don't need your services anymore. I'm calling to cancel the contract."

"You called to fire me?"

"Would you have preferred a text? An email?"

"I would prefer you weren't firing me!"

I'm going to try a different approach. Your approach isn't working, Ari."

"You think this is my fault? I've tried everything up to begging to get you parts! I'm going to level with you, Koryn. You aren't what most agencies are looking for."

"Why? Give me reasons!"

"Every role you want is the exact opposite of who and *how* you are and I can't change you."

I don't know what to say. I end the call, painfully aware of the truth of his words, but grateful for them. It's exactly what I needed to hear to push me one step closer to my escalator.

It's easy enough to find an image of her online. She's already a household name, even after only a few months of fame. The internet sleuths have dug into her background and revealed to the watching world some unsurprising information. Sandi was born perfect from head to toe and with a silver spoon in her mouth. Her family was privileged generations back, coming from old money and older values. She owned several houses, multiple cars. I don't have any of those things. I was born okay, but developed scoliosis as a kid, something only years of physical therapy fixed. That same medical treatment cost money and stress and was, according to both of my parents during their least fine moments, the reason they divorced. Where we were poor, we became poorer. I was raised surrounded by debt and taught how to spend what wasn't mine.

Sandi was Ivy League educated. I barely graduated high school. I can't even earn my first chip in A.A. But that failure gives me an idea. The Serenity Prayer taught me to change the things I can. Even on an escalator, you start on the bottom step.

What are the things I can change? My hair and eye color. My waistline, wardrobe, and social life. Half measures have availed us nothing. With some focus, I can change roles in my story. I can be her and I can reach the top.

"Where is it?" I screech to the room as I dig through the pile of junk mail—coupons, letters from local realtors, and ads for area landscapers—to find an envelope with a little window in its corner. I can feel the outline of the hard plastic through the paper and I carefully open the top flap to reveal the shiny, silver rectangle hot glued to the letter within. A platinum card for a future platinum blonde, my one-way ticket to success. Months ago I'd been pre-approved for some exorbitant amount with an equally high interest rate and signed-up for it as an emergency credit line. I dial the activation number off the sticker covering the front of the card. It's the last one, I promise myself that. I'll never open another credit line again, but this is important. This is an emergency. This is the rest of my life! I'm willing to pay the cost for beauty. I'll give up a pound of flesh, pints of beer, and my entire frumpy wardrobe just for a shot at glory. My tax guy told me once that I can write off things like this, stuff related to my profession. I'd say this qualifies as a career move.

I peck the card number into the payment screen, its maiden voyage in the form of an online order for frost blue contacts color-matched using over twenty different photos of Sandi's eyes. There's plenty to do while I wait the two days they'll take to arrive.

At the drugstore, hundreds of women with thick, shiny hair smile at me from their boxes. I can't find the right tone of blonde on any of their heads. Not one of them screams 'Sandi' because she'd never buy boxed dye. She was a salon girl. I move a few aisles down and grab the meal replacement shakes that I know will taste like chalk, but will give me the fast weight loss required to fit the part.

Down the street I see the answer to my hair woes, The Sip and Shear, a hip, wine-serving salon. The modern decor and the chic women inside intimidate me, but they can give me what I need if I can just manage to ask for it. I walk in with my fingers crossed and approach the receptionist.

"We don't take walk-ins," a petite brunette barks from behind the crescent-shaped desk, her eyes stuck on the pages of a gossipy celebrity magazine. Sandi stares at me from the cover.

Old me would turn around and head back to the bar for consolation at the bottom of a cup, but Sandi wouldn't be turned away. I focus on her face in print, inhale, and speak slowly to channel her confidence.

"I'm here to schedule an appointment."

The receptionist looks up. "Okay. That's different. What are you looking for?"

"I want whoever can make me that blonde." I point to the cover of the magazine. "That's the look I'm after."

The brunette checks the cover, stands up, and leans over the desk to whisper, "Monica has been super sad since Sandi stopped coming. She used to get her hair done here."

"I had no idea," I say, even though yesterday I'd read this was Sandi's regular salon.

"Maybe it'll be good for Monica. She's got an opening this afternoon."

"I'll take it!" I shriek, causing the girl behind the desk to jump. "Sorry, sorry. What time?"

"Give me your name and be back in about forty minutes."

"Koryn, with a 'k' and a 'y'," I explain. "See you soon."

Almost an hour. It's enough time for me to second-guess myself about the makeover. I end up a few blocks down, standing in front of Lauren, sweating from the walk and my nerves.

"You're up early. I can still smell yesterday's booze on you."

"I need a shot."

"Koryn, no. I won't let you day drink. You know that."

"Just one, for courage."

"Oh yeah? For what are we emboldening you?"

"Something drastic with my hair, for a character I'm auditioning to play. Come on. I don't want to be late for the appointment."

"I hope I don't regret this." Lauren reaches back for the Jagermeister, but I stop her.

"Do you have something less caloric? I'm trying to lose weight too."

She eyes me. "'*Caloric*?' What has gotten into you? You're like a new person."

"Not completely new. I can't stop drinking altogether, so I'm making a change."

"Right. No cold turkey, just room temperature vodka then?"

"Perfect." I hand her the new card, which she turns over and over in her hands.

"I don't know how you got approved for this, but it looks cool. Even has some weight to it."

"I'll take the bill. I don't want to keep it open."

"Wow. Words I never thought I'd hear you say."

Back at the salon, I step up to sit in Monica's chair and its narrow seat hugs my hips so tightly that I worry about escaping it once the job is done. It's clearly made for smaller people, with not even a nod to accessibility. Monica brings me a glass of red wine, chattering about how it was part of Sandi's ritual for her appointments. I sip it politely while she eyes my mid-brown, shade-above-honey hair in the mirror.

"Trish said you're after Sandi's look?"

"She's the perfect blonde."

"There's certainly truth in that, but most women spend hundreds on appointments attempting to reach your radiating shade of golden brown. You're lucky to have it as your natural color. Are you sure you want to suck the life out of it?"

I want to ask her about her dreams, if she plans on always standing behind someone else for the rest of her life, helping them reach theirs. "I've heard great things about your work," I choose to say instead. "If anyone can do her look justice, it's you."

She smirks. "Another fact." Unable to back down from a challenge to uphold her reputation, Monica drags the comb against my scalp. My drink-laden brain sloshes back and forth in my skull, a buoy on a turbulent sea. I fall into the sway as she separates chunks of hair for the bleach.

Sometime later she spins me around for the reveal. If I look through the extra weight and beyond my brown eyes, I can already see Sandi looking back.

"I don't miss the honey one bit. I love it!"

"If you plan on keeping this look, you'll need to make an appointment in three weeks or so for your roots."

"Of course! What do I owe you?"

"Trish will take care of that up front, but take your time."

I lose myself in the mirror, transfixed by my improving image, until Monica taps my shoulder and points to the clock. Fifteen minutes have gone.

"I didn't think you'd be so pleased. I've got my next appointment though. I'll need the chair."

"I'm so sorry!" I pry myself from my reflection and the seat with which my thighs have begun to merge. Regardless of that struggle, I hold my head high and head to the front to pay.

After swiping my card, Trish lifts the celebrity magazine up near my face. "Perfect match. Monica truly works miracles."

The blonde works its own miracles immediately. On my

errands, the cashier at the grocery store chats me up, pissing off the customers in line behind me and a stranger offers to help me with my bags in the parking lot. I head to a gym to sign up for a membership and the employee gives me an additional discount because, he says, he likes my smile, something that would never happen to me before. I'm used to being overlooked and taking the long way around, the hard road, but the blonde hair is a beacon clearing an easier path.

Two days later I tear open the box holding the next step in my metamorphosis. The contacts stare up at me from their safe, little container, icy pools penetrating right through me even though they're yet to belong to anyone. I place them and struggle a bit through the sensation of having something on my eyes and when the waiting is long enough I force them open.

"Holy shit. No way." The eyes make all the difference. I'm tempted to call off the diet and let this blonde-haired, blue-eyed version of me exist just fine, but I'm committed to the work it'll take. I can't stop short. Sandi wouldn't.

I take the card to a few boutiques, referencing her photographs for brands and colors. I can't try anything because I choose her size, the size I'll shrink to after many of the workouts I'm about to start.

"All right, Koryn! Are you ready for your first session?" The trainer jumps around with no obvious direction. I don't follow.

"No."

"That won't do. You wouldn't be here if you aren't ready! Are you ready?" He switches to jumping jacks, which mechanically make more sense, but are no more appealing than the previous movement.

"I don't want to jump around like that."

"Why are you here?"

"Ugh, I want to fit into the clothes in my closet."

"That's good! Bad news is you're going to have to jump around like this to do that. These are some warm ups to reintroduce your body to movement."

The warmups take an hour and I don't die, but I regret the decision a day later when I can't sit on the toilet without my thighs screaming in agony.

The next three weeks pass in a blur of increasingly difficult workouts and an aggressive dating circuit, punctuated only by the joy of forcing down the meal replacement shakes. Slowly I collect more images of Sandi, from her youth, her time in college, and in present day, and tack them on my living room wall in a makeshift mood board to inspire me.

I swipe right for Margarita Mondays with Matt, Lance, and Dave, Taco Tuesdays with Chad, Stephen, and Steve, Well Wednesdays with two different Anthonys, speed dating through Thirsty Thursdays with Erik, Ben, Liam, and others whose names aren't worth remembering. I make so much small talk during the weekdays that I am useless for singing on Karaoke Fridays. I try almost every bar and almost every type of guy, some multiple times, but none of the men anywhere seem good enough for her.

After all the effort, I do lose twenty-five pounds and gain access to the still-tagged clothing hanging in my closet. I wake up a little different every day. Ari eventually stops calling and gives up on emailing me as well. Letting go of him feels like one of the final weights lifted.

I turn the corner of my usual haunt and my heart thumps faster. The building hasn't changed at all in my three weeks away from it. The same outdated drink specials crust and flake off the windows, the same lipstick-stained cigarette butts stick in the cracks where the building meets the sidewalk. The bar is a chick in sweatpants that I don't need to impress, but I feel nervous about facing Lauren. I've been cheating on her with other bartenders, giving her tips to other wallets. My absence has cost her money.

I walk in and straight to the bar. She looks up and down and back up in a double take before smiling. I've never before seen anyone so happy to see me. For a moment I wish she was looking that way at the old me, instead of this mimic of a woman that I've become.

"Well if it isn't Miss Witness Protection herself. I barely recognized you! Where'd you go?"

I'm ashamed to say I hate myself so much I'd remake my entire appearance in someone else's image. She offers me an out.

"I'm guessing you got the part? The one you said you had a good feeling about the last time I saw you?"

"What?" I ask as I'd honestly forgotten the lie.

"When I got you that vodka shot before you went to the hair salon, remember?"

"Oh! Yeah, yeah. Sorry, it's been a busy few weeks. I'm doing a character study. It's part of my process. I needed to change it up. I wasn't finding the right roles, like you said."

She squeals, pulls her hands into fists, and stomps her feet, something I've never seen her do before. It's the type of girlish excitement I wasn't sure she was capable of. I don't even have a process. I've never had one.

"I knew something good must have happened! You're not too good for us then, are you? I wasted more than a few drinks expecting you to show up."

"Sorry about that. I told you I was dating, yeah?"

"Looking for Mr. Right, right?"

"Yes, well," I throw my head to the left, my blonde tresses casually following, signaling her to look down the barstools, "it's not exactly the pick of the litter in here."

"Fuck you!" the drunken man at the end of the bar yells. "I could fuck you if I wanted."

"Mr. *Right Now* proves my point. I had to try some other bars to increase my chances of finding him."

"The regulars here aren't all aging drunkards, some of them are young, functioning alcoholics like you, Koryn." She laughs, but the term stings no matter how much truth surrounds it. I feign a smile and resist taking another sip of my beer just so I can prove her wrong.

"I'm not just looking for any guy. I'm seeking a very specific type."

"Give me the deets. I can keep a lookout, play Cupid for you."

Before I can reply, Sandi's on TV again and my eyes drift and stick to the screen.

"You just can't take your eyes off of her. Maybe it's time to swing for the other team? It's super easy to change your preferences on that app you use. And you've already changed everything else about you. Maybe you need a woman."

"I've told you, I don't *want* her."

"Then what is it? Why are you so captivated?" A look of revelation covers Lauren's face. "This makeover wasn't for a job at all, was it?"

"No." The shame reddens my cheeks.

"Well? What is it then?"

"I guess...I wish I *was* her."

"Are you delusional? I'm sorry. That was harsh. You want to be this woman?"

I backpedal to an answer I think might somehow sound more acceptable to her. "No. No. What I meant to say is that I want to be wanted by a man who wants a woman like her. I can't exactly put that on a dating profile."

"Well you're well on your way to getting that. You're a downright doppelgänger. I think that's enough for tonight." She grabs my drink and dumps it into the sink behind her.

"I wasn't done with that."

"That's how I know. You aren't even drunk. This obsession is a month in the making. I fucking wish I could blame this on your drinking problem. I'm disappointed."

"Lauren."

"It's time for you to go. Don't worry about the bill."

"You told me to find an escalator. I think she's it."

"Learn to love yourself and get better idols, Koryn. Don't be surprised when you get what you're asking for."

Lauren walks away from me to check on other patrons. I leave the bar, feeling more sober than when I arrived.

Ari stops me outside, but not because he recognizes me, because he doesn't. It's the same way he stopped me years ago when I was a stranger to him, when I was younger and prettier. He could have been watching me through the window, waiting for me to close my tab and leave. He's a shark like that.

"Have you ever thought about acting?" he asks, business card in his extended hand.

"I've already got one of those. Hasn't gotten me much."

He lowers his hand and leans closer as though to examine my features.

"Wow, Koryn, is that you? Is *this* the different approach? I can't believe it! You should have done this years ago! I can work with this! This will get us to Hollywood!"

"Us? I fired you. I'm representing myself."

"How's that going? Any leads?"

I scoff. "Wouldn't you like to know!" The feeling of power lasts but a moment before I burst into tears, because I'm still single and out of work, and my bartender has broken up with me. I'm drink-, dick-, and director-less, despite stealing Sandi's entire look. Some escalator she turned out to be.

"Hey, it's okay." He lightly pats my shoulder.

"No, it's not okay, Ari! If I don't get cast, I'll have to declare bankruptcy!"

"Give me another chance. I'll pay for new headshots; you don't look anything like the old ones. And I won't bill you for any of my legwork unless we secure a job. "

I wipe my eyes. "You've said that before."

"This time it's different because I know you can book one."

"Sweet talking isn't your strong suit, Ari."

"You're right. I'm a man of action, not words."

He takes a photo of me with his cell phone.

"That'll do in the meantime. I'll be in touch!" He whisks away, like a man with places to be. I'm flattered, but annoyed that he didn't give me a chance to check my makeup.

At home, I head straight to the vodka in my freezer and drink until I forget that instead of paying off, my efforts have cost me my only friendship.

The crystal clear, blue waters of my irises turn to murky puddles as I pluck the contacts from my eyes. I lean in and study my scalp to find that my roots are growing in. The gig is up, the charade over. My fraudulent beauty will soon be discovered.

I check the balance on my newest credit card and see there's enough left for another appointment with the salon and maybe one more night out before I cut my losses and fade back into debt and obscurity.

As early as hungover me can wake, I venture back to The Sip and Shear. Trish works the desk once again. This time, she stands to greet me.

"Does Monica have an opening?" I ask, waiting to be berated for suggesting an appointment on the spot.

The girl smiles warmly. "I'm sooo sorry, she's not in today, but I'm sure Stacy can squeeze you in no problem. Stacy?" Trish yells toward the back of the salon.

Stacy shampoos my hair aggressively, clearly unhappy with another head on her schedule. My bent neck is the only thing keeping vomit from rising out of my sour stomach from all the vigorous scrubbing. I move to the chair at her station and my slim hips slide comfortably into the narrow seat, a non-scale victory I wasn't expecting.

"Thanks for getting me in on such short notice."

"Uh huh. What do you want?"

"The roots, they won't do."

"They're barely showing. Most women go a bit longer

before putting their hair through more damage."

"I'm an actress. They can't show at all."

Stacy rolls her eyes in the mirror and mouths my words 'I'm an actress' while sneering. She either doesn't remember or doesn't care that I can see her.

"Look, Monica told me to come in as soon as I saw the roots."

I wonder if Stacy treated Sandi this way. The name drop of Stacy's boss seems to work, since she grabs the bottle of bleach and gets to work in helping me sell the lie.

My cell rings and it's Ari.

"You want to get that? Might be an important call. Maybe it's your agent."

"Actually that's exactly who it is," I hiss. "I'll call him back when you're done."

High on the bleach fumes, I come to a realization. I've been going about it all wrong. Sandi wouldn't drink in any of the bars I've been to. She'd go somewhere fancy, a place where the heads she turns would be attached to bodies of power with big jobs and bigger bank accounts. She'd go somewhere with a dress code. She'd go to the Sip and Shear of bars. She'd go to Flute.

Later in the night, neck sore from Stacy's callous jostling, I stand outside the only wine bar in the city dressed in a form-fitted, black dress and red high heels. I check my reflection in the door and adjust what needs adjusting, primping both my gentle waves and my tits. The room quiets as I enter, the waitstaff stop mid-stride, the bartenders, mid-pour, and the guests all turn to watch me. I feel like the leading lady of a play, moving to center stage or a butterfly freshly emerged from its chrysalis to take its first flight.

I pick a seat in the middle of the room and order Sandi's usual, a bitter house red. The other patrons can't seem to take their eyes off me as I drain my first glass.

A man stares over the chasm created by the circular shape of the bar. He looks at me with hunger. The dim lights darken the shadows of his strong cheekbones and deepen the black of his three-piece suit. He's a definite improvement from the men I've spent the last three weeks entertaining and before I know it, he's in the seat beside me.

"I have to say, your hair looks incredible."

"Thank you. It's recently been redone."

"I'm Dan."

"Koryn."

"And what are you drinking, Koryn?"

"The house red."

"Always a good choice. Hey, if you don't mind me saying, you remind me of someone I used to know."

"Yeah?'

"Yeah. I think the entire bar is thinking the same thing. Sandi used to come here a lot. I'm sure you've heard of her?"

I smile. "Hasn't everyone?"

"It's a little eerie, actually. How striking the resemblance is. If they ever make a movie about what happened, you could play her."

"That's perfect. I'm an actress. I love a challenging role."

"Sandi wanted to pursue acting, but she was so busy with the fundraising and the charity work. Really an incredible woman. She wanted to be a nurse too."

"I've considered a career in medicine," I lie, becoming

the most interesting woman alive, one line at a time in a bid to keep him next to me.

Dan stares off into the distance until he catches the eyes of the bartender and signals him to us.

"I'll have another Jack Daniels and she'll have another of the house red."

The bartender hangs around a moment longer. "It's last call, which means the last chance to change your mind. There's no backing out of this decision."

"Look at her," Dan says to him. "This is a woman who knows what she wants."

The bartender agrees by silently taking the order.

"Crazy! Sandi loved red wine too!" Dan's eyes bulge in a frantic mix of disbelief and amazement.

"What a lovely coincidence," I coo softly to hide my involvement in the collusion. You can find almost anything on the internet, including aged reviews from happy customers recommending their drink of choice, though Sandi's five stars for the red blend seems a bit of a steep praise for my palette.

For the rest of the night, I listen to Dan talk. His lips are beautiful when he speaks, regardless of how many of the words coming out are about her. We drink and laugh and my giddiness over his attention has me floating. His drunkenness has him calling me Sandi by closing time.

The lights turn up slightly, a gentle nudge for us to pay our tabs and go. Dan gets my drinks.

He stands next to me outside, the night air sobering him enough to realize I'm not her. "It's a sad kind of deja vu. You know, Sandi always had a driver waiting."

"Must be nice to have a driver," I mumble, becoming slightly disillusioned over the fun I thought I had.

"Can I walk you home? It can be a rough neighborhood."

I think of the blocks ahead and can't stand to hear him say her name one more time. "No, I'll be fine. I'm always fine."

"If you say so. I'm here every Saturday. I'd love to see you again. Be careful!"

"Goodnight. Thank you for a nice evening."

I watch him walk down the street into the darkness. Before, when I was ugly, nobody warned me about how dangerous the world was. When I wasn't desirable, it was safe to walk the streets alone at any hour, in any neighborhood. Did Sandi live in fear? Was the world waiting for her to let down her guard? To be alone so it could gobble her up? I inhale and my neck aches. My ten block walk is uneventful and peaceful until I'm nearly home and Ari calls my cell.

"If we're going to be working together, you can't avoid my calls."

"I was at the salon earlier and I've been out since."

"Please tell me you didn't get rid of that blonde."

"Just got my roots done. Why?"

"You've got a job!"

"Without auditioning?"

"I showed them the photo I took with my phone. They want to meet you just to be sure you're a good fit, but they said you're the closest to character they've seen."

"Ari, that's amazing! When?"

"Tomorrow. Bright and early. If you've been drinking, don't have any more tonight."

"Things are finally coming together for me. I can't

believe it."

"This could be your breakout role, Koryn. I've got a feeling."

I have a feeling too, like I'm not alone on the sidewalk. I have a feeling of someone following me. I resist the urge to turn and look and bring my focus back to Ari.

"What kind of job is it?"

"It's a little macabre, but you can decline the offer if it's just too dark. If I were you, I'd take it. The exposure will be huge."

"Are you going to tell me what it is?"

I feel the gap between myself and my mystery tail close. My safety, like water in a bath, displaced by a body. My heart begins to race. Ari's call cuts in and out.

"The wom--, the blonde. Um, hold -n."

The noise of shuffling papers crinkles through the speaker of my phone.

"I had to plug my phone in. Sandi Brook. Sounds like a fake name. The dead woman."

"She's missing, Ari, not dead."

"Toe-may-toh, toe-mah-toh. You know who I mean? You've seen her on the news?"

I see her in the mirror. "Yeah."

"The job is some kind of re-enactment. They want you to play her. They think it'll help the public remember details from the night she disappeared. They've already aired a couple for some of the other missing women. Linda and April. Consider those homework. I've got to go. I've emailed you the info."

"Wait! Can you stay on the phone? Ari?"

He doesn't reply because he's already hung up.

I keep my phone out, ready to dial an emergency line.

Two more blocks to go.

Weakened by malnutrition and the unintentional vodka wine cocktail hitting my bloodstream, I slow and my shadow gains on me. The faster I try to move, the more sluggish I become, as though I'm accelerating on an empty tank. What will they say about me when I go missing? When they go to my apartment to investigate my disappearance? What will they say when they find the shrine to Sandi's excellence and the evidence of my mediocrity and desperation, forever immortalized in colored contact lens packaging and a recycling bin full of empty weight loss shake bottles? Who will they know to look for when every picture is of the old me? How will Lauren describe me? *Like Sandi, but with problems*? Will anyone's head turn for Ari's shaky cell phone photo of me as it's plastered all over the news? Will they use my name or will they relegate me to the corner of 'another woman', a Sandi lookalike gone missing.

I hear the *whoosh* of something before it hits my head. The force of the blow sends me twirling around to face a man. He's older than the police sketches made him out to be, shorter and chubbier too. Grey flecks his hair and glitters under the streetlamp. There's nothing tall, dark, and handsome, nothing chiseled, about him. I've seen him before at several of the bars, but he looked right through me and I, him. Is this the kind of man who wanted Sandi? If so, who am I to disallow him wanting me? So what if he isn't perfect. I still have stretch marks etched into my ass cheeks, proof I haven't always been this small. I'm still an alcoholic. I can taste the wine on my tongue as my mouth begins to fill with blood. It's too late to turn back, because he whacked my head open. Who knew my big break would be a major fracture to my skull?

Once they check my bank account, and subsequently, the surveillance video from Flute, they'll see me dressed in my best outfit, having fun with Dan. They'll interview him. They'll waste time considering him as a suspect since he knew Sandi as well. They'll say we're his type and the man in front of me now will get away.

He swings the bat again and I'm down on the ground, writhing, turning my head to find the light of a nearby streetlamp.

"I found you," I say with blood-gargled, delirious triumph. I cough and blood runs down the sides of my face. It must look amazing in contrast to the blonde. I scrutinize his blurring features with my fading vision. His eyes wobble and move back to the right place on his face. Blood flows through my eyelashes and drips over my frost-colored eyes, daring a final curtain call.

He lifts me into a truck and pulls the seatbelt across my abdomen. I laugh at my status as precious cargo. I'm bleeding out through a gash in my head, but heaven forbid I die in a car accident. It's my death on his terms. Somewhere I've lost one of my red heels.

He finally speaks once he's in the driver's seat. "Saw you walking around. Thought I'd seen a ghost. But that ain't right. Not much of her left to see, I reckon."

"Sandi?"

He nods.

I think of her wine-stained lips, coated in the clotted blood of our mirror image deaths. "Is she where we're going?"

"It's a long drive, but worth it. I have the perfect farmhouse for you."

ACKNOWLEDGMENTS

I have first to thank my greatest love, Jonathan Butcher. You've done more from a distance as a partner to support my success than anyone standing right in front of me has prior. This collection is born from countless hours, many of them spent with you on our late night writing sessions on Skype. You've taught me so much of what I didn't know about being a good writer and your confidence in me propels me forward on days I feel I could stop in place and never write again. Thank you for believing in me.

To all the women who volunteered to die in this collection, thank you for lending your names to a worthy cause.

To the incredible writers I am fortunate enough to call friends, thank you for being excited and exhausted by the same craft. I often look to your example and find comfort in our shared experience.

To my family and friends for understanding the time and attention this takes, thank you.

And thank you to the staff at Barnes and Noble in Alderwood, WA. The faith you have in my abilities is invaluable.

To Crypticon Seattle and related groups for providing the venue and event at which I debut my books.

Finally, I thank you, dear reader, for lending your eyes, your time, and your mind to my ideas.

-Michelle

ABOUT THE AUTHOR

Michelle is a lover of the macabre who prefers earl grey tea, October, and people who say goodbye on the phone. Her dreams are so real she sometimes can't figure out what has really happened to her. When she isn't writing, Michelle enjoys weightlifting, dark beer, web design, singing and playing guitar, watching horror movies, and playing video games. She is afraid of the dark.

She is the author of the novel *When the Dead* and the novella *Mistakes I Made During the Zombie Apocalypse*, three other short stories collections: *Last Night While You Were Sleeping, When You Find Out What You're Made Of,* and *Once Upon a Time When Things Turned Out Okay,* a co-author of *The Spread* which she wrote with her twin sister, and a co-editor of *GIVE: An Anthology of Anatomical Entries.* Her short stories are featured in several anthologies. She has one nonfiction work on toxic relationships based on personal experience called *The Murk of Us.* Find her on Instagram and TikTok.

ABOUT WHEN THE DEAD BOOKS

When the Dead Books is a small book company run by owner and author Michelle von Eschen. We bring horror, sci-fi, and fantasy fiction from indie writers to you.

WHEN THE DEAD BOOKS

[QUIET, LITERARY HORROR AND APOCALYPTIC FICTION]

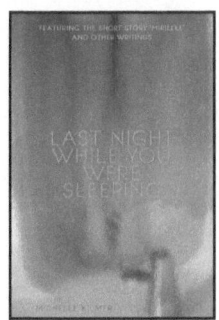

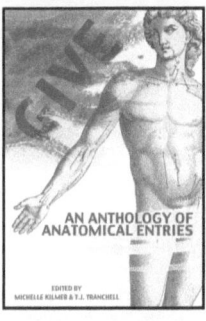

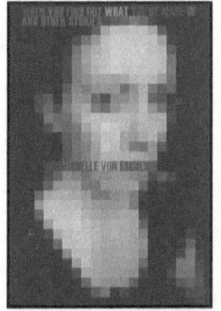

www.whenthedead.com   facebook.com/whenthedead